A CASE FOR BRUTUS LLOYD

Dr. Brutus Lloyd was no more than four feet ten inches tall, an amazingly gnome-like man. The most surprising thing about him was his deep bass voice. A brilliant scientist and criminologist, his unorthodox methods caused consternation to Inspector Branson of the New York City Police when: an accident caused a mining engineer to see into 'another world'; four scientists were murdered for their collective brainpower, and when dinosaurs were seen on the outskirts of a village . . .

JOHN RUSSELL FEARN

A CASE FOR BRUTUS LLOYD

EDITED BY
PHILIP HARBOTTLE

Complete and Unabridged

LINFORD
Leicester

First published in Great Britain

First Linford Edition
published 2011

Copyright © 1940, 1942 by John Russell Fearn
Copyright © 2011 by Philip Harbottle

British Library CIP Data

Fearn, John Russell, *1908 – 1960.*
A case for Brutus Lloyd.- -
(Linford mystery library)
1. New York (N. Y.). Police Dept.- -Fiction.
2. Detective and mystery stories.
3. Large type books.
I. Title II. Series
823.9′12–dc22

ISBN 978–1–44480–608–3

Published by
F. A. Thorpe (Publishing)
Anstey, Leicestershire

Set by Words & Graphics Ltd.
Anstey, Leicestershire
Printed and bound in Great Britain by
T. J. International Ltd., Padstow, Cornwall

This book is printed on acid-free paper

1

BLIND VISION

1

Strange accident

Ralph Marshall never knew what really happened. One minute he was carrying on his normal work as mining engineer, supervising the drilling of the giant shaft which it was hoped would one day pass under the Atlantic Ocean from the United States to Britain — and the next there was the sound of smashing concussion in his ears and blinding light before his eyes. He stumbled and fell amidst a rain of tumbling rocks, props, and underpinnings . . .

Voices merged out of darkness. Sounds of instruments clinking and tinkling in glass vessels. Ralph Marshall felt throbbing pain throughout his body. He stirred and winced. A nurse's voice spoke to him gently.

'Just relax, Mr. Marshall. You'll be all right.'

He obeyed perforce, piecing together the past events. There was a wadding of bandages across his eyes, tight binding round his arm. It felt as though his leg were in a plaster cast. But his biggest worry was the dark — total, pitchy. Had his sight gone? Had it been destroyed in the mine blowout? That was something he did not dare to think about.

But as hours and days slid by, as days slipped into weeks, as the rest of his body healed and his eyes did not, he began to realize the truth. He realized it all the more clearly when the bandages were unwound from his face and he raised his eyelids. The darkness remained unchanged.

'Doc!' he shouted hoarsely, gripping the hand that held him. 'Doc, what's wrong with me? I can't see! Everything's . . . black!'

The voice of Dr. Talford Flint, chief doctor of the hospital, sounded as impartial as ever.

'Just sit here, Mr. Marshall, while we take a look at you.'

Ralph fumbled for the high backed

chair and fell into it, sat motionless, breathing hard, staring into the abyss. He heard the whirr and buzz of electrical machinery, the mutter of voices in consultation.

Suddenly, sharp questions stabbed from the dark.

'Can you see this? No? Well — this? No reaction? Hm . . . '

More muttering. Dr. Flint's voice rose higher than the others with its sharp, acid sting.

'The eyes react normally, I tell you! Optic nerves are quite in order. Maybe a case of temporary shock. Nonsense, man!' he scoffed at somebody. 'Nonsense! Cannot be the brain-centres . . . '

Ralph sprang up suddenly. 'Would somebody mind telling me what the devil's going on in here?' he demanded, almost with a touch of hysteria. 'Stop cackling, can't you, and let me have the truth!'

Flint's voice replied, monotonously calm. 'If we could tell you what is wrong with your eyes, Mr. Marshall, we would do so — but we cannot! They answer to every one of our tests, and for that reason you should be able to see. That you cannot see is something we are unable to explain. It's — it's temporary blindness and will pass off eventually, just as snow-blindness does.'

'And supposing it doesn't?' Ralph stood mastering himself. He went on desperately, 'There must be somebody who can diagnose, surely?'

'In this room are the best experts in optics, Mr. Marshall,' Flint retorted. 'Your firm insisted on the best possible specialists to examine you . . . That has been done. It is simply a case of your eyes not answering to normal optical laws, that's all. We can do nothing more to help you — but keep on calling nonetheless so we can note an improvement the moment it appears. We'll keep thorough track of your case, of course.'

Ralph smiled bitterly. Thorough track! That was the last thing he could imagine this cold-blooded fish, Talford Flint, ever doing. Though he had never yet seen him he had long since summed up the man's nature from his ruthless voice.

Ralph said quietly, 'Well, thanks . . . ' A hand caught his arm. He could tell by the cool draught when he was in the main passage. Then another hand caught him — a strong hand he immediately recognized, that of Ed Rutter, his assistant engineer on the Shaft.

'Good to see you around on your pins again, Ralph.' Ed's voice was genuinely pleased. 'How's tricks?'

'Not so hot, I guess.' Ralph fingered his dark glasses and gave a brief account of the medico's edict as they passed down the steps together.

'They're crazy!' was Ed's summing up. 'I dragged you out of that blowout myself. You got a smack on the head, a cracked leg, and a burned arm — nothing more. You'll be okay, don't worry. In the meantime you can hitch to me. I'll keep the flies off you.'

'That,' Ralph said quietly, 'is the part I don't like. You know I'm not built to rely on other people. I've got to do things myself, with my own two hands — Oh, hell, why did this have to happen to me?'

Ed said philosophically, 'I suppose

things can happen to the best of us. Stop worrying, man. Just keep on digging in with me at the apartment until you get right again.'

Ralph gripped the strong hand gratefully. He needed no words to convince him of the tough, red-haired engineer's loyalty. Ed Rutter was the sort of man who'd give his right arm in defence of somebody he really liked.

There was a long silence between them after that. Then after a while Ralph noted from the increasing roar of traffic that they had come into the heart of New York. In his mind's eye he could see the way to their apartment, could also see the three-mile distance of crisscrossing streets that led to the vast excavations at the Shaft entrance. Three times a shaft had been attempted, and still it was incomplete.

For Ralph all that was over now, he felt. He had to pattern a new sort of life. He had money saved, plenty of it. The firm had intimated they would grant him a life pension. Did that imply that they thought he would never . . . ? He crushed the thought from his mind.

Over the meal in the apartment Ed's voice went on in forced cheeriness. Ralph did not listen to all the things he said. His thoughts were on his immediate predicament. Then he started violently as the alarm clock went off — that infernal clock, always going off at the wrong time, moving itself along the mantelshelf by the very vibration of its ringing.

Ed leapt for it, jammed on the silencer.

'Tell you what,' he said, turning again. 'Why not let me go and get you one of those dogs? You know — eyes of the blind, and all that. I don't want to rub it in, but you could get about.'

'Thanks — no,' Ralph answered curtly. 'I haven't given up hope yet, Ed. A dog to run around with me would sort of make me feel tied down. I'll get better — somehow.'

'But until you do — '

'Oh, quit worrying me, can't you?' Ralph blazed.

Ed relaxed and lighted a cigarette. Ralph crushed out his own cigarette with strong, knotty fingers. Thereafter he drummed on the table with a definite desperation of spirit.

★ ★ ★

In the ensuing days Ralph Marshall debated many courses of action. Should he just vanish from sight? Should he put an end to himself? He did not consider it would be cowardice: he was a firm believer in ridding the world of useless material, organic or inorganic. He might . . . No: there was always the thought he might recover.

A week passed. In that week his moods were those of a man driven to distraction. He had periods of smouldering calm; then he flew into berserk rages, ranted, finally apologized — and Ed Rutter came from and went to work on the Shaft with calm, cheerful understanding. He knew only too well the ordeal his dynamic, energetic friend was undergoing.

Then something happened! One of the mornings when he was left alone as usual Ralph noticed something queer. There was a puncture in the abyss of darkness

— a tiny hole of light!

Ralph's whole being suddenly exploded with hysterical delight. He sat staring at that hole, rolling his eyes to make sure, but whichever way he turned his eyes the hole remained. It was perhaps as large as a pea. Straining to the utmost, he tried to analyze what he saw. He held his hand before his face, but for some reason could not see any trace of his hand at all in the hole. Not that that discouraged him: he remained confident that he would do so before long.

He phoned the news to Ed down in the Shaft. That evening they had a celebration supper on the strength of it. From then on Ed was as keenly interested as Ralph himself in the gradual expansion of that hole day by day. Once or twice Ralph toyed with the idea of going back to the hospital for an examination, then decided against it. Better to get himself wholly well before being tested and proven all right for work again.

The hole grew. With the growth came a sense of dawning wonder to Ralph. Four days later it was large enough to encompass a quarter of his vision, but he was not looking at anything in the apartment! He walked in bewilderment from room to room, but he never saw a familiar thing, and certainly failed to observe the furniture with which he collided. And yet the scene changed as he moved about. He saw things that in their partial state, he could not understand or reconcile. Otherwise it seemed he was as blind as ever. He still could not see his waving hands in front of his face, could not see a sign of anything immediately around him.

His first hopes began to diminish, but not entirely. There was definite interest in watching the development of returning sight — though what sort of a world he was going to look into he dared not imagine.

He purposely kept most of the truth from Ed, only told him enough to let him believe he was recovering very gradually. In another week the vision was completely clear to Ralph, and sitting on the divan in the living room one morning with his dark glasses off, he gazed — and gazed.

He was alone in the apartment; he knew that — but instead of being in the apartment he was apparently sitting on the sidewalk of a tremendously long main street. He gazed down it steadily, remarking the absolute clarity of detail.

People passed him constantly but never glanced at him — busy people, men and women, just as he had always known them, except that their attire was rather different to prevailing fashion. It struck him as curious, but here and there people came straight toward him and passed on — through him! He was convinced of it after a while, and the sensation was startling.

He studied this particular section of city carefully. It was not familiar in the least, was apparently a mass of rearing towers. Here and there were bullet-nosed rocket airplanes, far in advance of any known to modern civilization.

The buildings seemed to have millions of windows. Directional towers for aircraft were atop every edifice. There were car parks high in the air, floor upon floor, driven by endless belt systems. All ground space was devoted to traffic ways and open parks, with special sidewalks for pedestrians.

Even the traffic was peculiar. There was not a single recognizable make of automobile in sight, and what there were moved silently and swiftly. It was odd, Ralph reflected — in fact fantastic. He could see all this activity, which should have made the din of a super-modern city, yet all he could hear was the pounding tick of that old fashioned alarm clock on the mantel. He closed his eyes momentarily and the vision was shut out; but it was there again when he opened them once more.

His exact emotions were unfathomable. In one sense he was profoundly disappointed because he was obviously as blind as ever; yet in another he was aware of a feeling of triumph at being the dissociated observer of something bafflingly complex. This required study.

So to Ed Rutter he only gave brief reports and wore dark glasses whenever Ed was about. But week after week thereafter he studied the city by day and

14

night, the periods of daylight and darkness corresponding exactly with those of the normal world.

Among other things Ralph took advantage of Ed's suggestion. He got a dog. Thereby he was enabled to extend the scope of his activity. At first he was faced with considerable confusion. Walking down the main street in the other city, for instance, demanded walking through a New York emporium and leaving by the back entrance! To gain elevation and study the city properly he had to go to the top of New York's highest buildings.

Everywhere his dog unfailingly guided him. Everywhere the faces of the Others looked unseeingly at him. He was the invisible observer of a great, mysterious, busy world.

It was perhaps inevitable that the vision of this new world should affect Ralph with increasing force. His body was in the normal world, but sight was elsewhere! He got into the habit of calling to the people passing by him — and getting no answer of course — of repeating the various proclamations on the signs and posters he saw, all of them in an unknown language. He began to build up a small vocabulary, both from looking at newspapers over people's shoulders and watching the things they did, or the things they indicated, when they spoke. He became gradually adept in lip reading.

There was something else too. In this other plane matter was no barrier to him. He passed through walls and people as easily as people passed through him. Yet of course it was impossible for him to touch anything.

Ralph forgot his caution as time went on. His interest was utterly absorbed. On more than one occasion Ed was surprised to find him in the act of apparently talking to himself in unknown jargon, staring straight before him while he did it. It worried Ed not a little. He thought he took the right course when he reported the matter back to the hospital.

Accordingly the hospital contacted Ralph's firm. They in turn made arrangements, and one morning Dr. Flint himself and two other experts turned up at the apartment.

Once the brief examination was over Ralph sat in his bedroom, waiting, listening to the voices floating through the fanlight over the door.

'I cannot help but think he needs attention, gentlemen,' Ed was saying earnestly. 'Being left alone too much maybe. Probably affecting his mind. He talks to himself, does queer things. He even thinks at times that he is in a street when standing in this room!'

Ralph did not catch the answer, but he got to his feet and entered the living room suddenly. He sensed the sudden expectancy his arrival created.

'Gentlemen,' he said quietly, 'I think there is something you should know. I can see.' He took off his dark glasses. 'I see, but I do not see you! I do not even see New York. No, I see another world, another city, another race of people. At this very moment I am looking down the main street.'

Still there was silence.

'Well, have you nothing to say?' Ralph demanded. 'Aren't you even going to try and find out what is wrong? I suppose I should have told you this sooner, but I was waiting for you to tell *me*. Only you didn't! If you can't find out the truth then let me get a man who will. There's Dr. Brutus Lloyd, for instance. He was with me at college once — '

'I hardly think we need to consider the so called merits of Dr. Lloyd at this moment,' broke in Flint's curt voice. Then in a more conciliatory tone he went on, 'We are well able to take care of you, Mr. Marshall. If you will accompany us back to the hospital where we have all the instruments we will see what we can do.'

'It's obviously an optical defect,' Ralph said, as he put back his glasses and was helped into his coat. 'You know — embracing an angle in space which we cannot see under normal conditions. These other people do exist, and their city is much improved on ours.'

'Of course — of course.' Dr. Flint sounded as though he was humouring a lunatic.

Ralph was full of inner doubts as he was driven through the streets. Dimly through his dark glasses he could see apparent buildings whirling towards him, through which the car passed like vapour. The whole mad other-plane was careening round in dizzying circles. He felt himself sway a little when he finally alighted from the car. He was taken up in an elevator and seemed to rise up the face of a building. He became stationary half way up and fell into a chair. Once his glasses were removed he found himself gazing over a futuristic square with waving trees lining either side of it. Silent, as ever.

Then Dr. Flint said, 'Now for a few tests, Mr. Marshall.'

This time the tests were not entirely confined to the eyes. For an hour or more Ralph found himself taken from chair to chair, felt unseen instruments at work upon him, heard muttered consultations. Then at last Flint spoke out clearly.

'Mr. Marshall, our tests reveal no change whatever in your eyes since the previous examination. Whatever you believe you see cannot be at all connected with your eyes. It is, to be perfectly frank, the outcome of brain pressure from your accident. Delusions if you will. Once you asked for the truth — now you shall have it. So far as we can tell there is no chance of your eyes ever recovering sight. Further, the strange visions you speak of, together with the queer behavior noted by your friend Mr. Rutter lead us to one definite conclusion . . . '

'You mean you think I'm crazy?' Ralph snapped.

'We believe,' Flint said, 'that you would certainly be better under observation here until you lose your delusions. We can no doubt soon cure you. It is what your firm would wish.'

'Now listen!' Ralph exclaimed earnestly. 'You think I'm going insane. I tell you I'm as sane as you are, only my vision's gone haywire. Didn't it ever occur to any of you that a shock might cause the optic nerves to become hyper-sensitive or something?'

'Are you an optician, Mr. Marshall?' Flint inquired coldly.

'You know I'm not; but I have some scientific knowledge and I know plenty of things can happen to a person after a shock. Take — take lightning, for instance. Haven't you ever heard of people being able to see through solids after being struck by lightning? Is it not possible, then, that I — '

'We don't think so!' Flint broke in curtly. 'We are dealing with facts, not fantasies. You require treatment and close supervision, examination by other specialists, in our psychopathic department.'

'But look here — '

'You may rest assured we are acting from the best interests,' Flint concluded implacably. Then aside, 'Attend to it!'

A door slammed.

Ralph swore openly, started to struggle as strong hands took hold of him obviously those of male nurses. Finally he gave up the battle as useless. His dark glasses were replaced on his nose and he was led out into the corridor. The next thing he knew he was in a room, alone.

He knew after a while that it was well furnished, comfortable enough — but his hands found bars on the windows and the door was securely locked. From rage his emotions changed to deep wonder. Flint must surely know he was *not* insane. Why, then, the captivity?

2

Dr. Brutus Lloyd

Once he realized how ruthlessly the medicos had put Ralph Marshall into virtual imprisonment, Ed Rutter's fury knew no bounds. He bitterly regretted ever having mentioned the matter.

He ranted and raved at the callous Dr. Flint, and got nowhere. He tried to make the newspapers take it up, but editors were chary of it. As a last hope Ed recalled the name of Dr. Brutus Lloyd, looked up his address and occupation from the directory. He was listed as a research chemist, but his degrees filled two small columns and other remarks spoke of proficiency in the fields of optics, physics, medicine, and criminology.

'In plain words, a dabbler,' Ed mused. 'Might do worse, though.'

So he tracked Dr. Lloyd down to his out-town house — a rather old fashioned place in its own grounds, well free of the city bustle yet connected with the metropolis by a wide main road.

Inside, as a manservant took his card, Ed found evidences of unexpected opulence about the residence. His feet sank into rich carpet; the walls were lined with armoury, costly brasses, rare antiques. Clearly Brutus Lloyd was not short of cash by any means.

The manservant came back noiselessly. 'If you will step into the laboratory, Mr. Rutter?'

Ed found himself conducted through a door at the end of the hall. He passed into one of the most completely equipped laboratories he had ever seen. The glass roof was fitted with slanted mirrors so that shadowless daylight was cast in every direction. For a while he stood looking round on beakers, retorts, electric engines, switchboards. Of Dr. Lloyd himself there seemed to be no sign — until suddenly a tiny figure came from behind a bench, wiping his hands down his smock.

For a moment Ed stared in surprise.

Lloyd was no more than four feet ten inches tall, an amazingly gnome-like man. He was not a dwarf or a freak, simply vest-pocket size. The most surprising thing about him was his head. It was squarish with a brow like a baby cliff, capped on top by a tuft of jet-black hair that permitted one lock to curl in a J down the immense forehead. The eyes were small and piercing, almost masked by black eyebrows and lashes. The face, though overbalanced by the brow, was powerful for all its smallness. Possibly Lloyd was forty; certainly no less.

'I presume you came for a reason other than to gape, Mr. Rutter?'

Brutus Lloyd's voice was the biggest shock of all. It was deep bass.

'I'm — I'm sorry, doctor,' Ed hastened to apologize. 'I sort of expected to — '

'To find a big man with a white beard dabbling in hellish alchemy?' Lloyd asked, with a babyish smile. 'Well you didn't, and I'm not . . . What's your trouble?'

'I believe you're a criminologist and scientist? Also connected with optics, physics, and medicine?'

'*Dolus versatur in generalibus*,' Lloyd rumbled. 'A snare lurks in generalities . . . Just what concern is it of yours what I do? What are you — a reporter? If so — out!'

'No — no, wait a minute. I want your help — from the criminal and optical side.'

'Really?' Lloyd stroked his forelock for a moment. Then with his sharp little eyes narrowed a little he said slowly, 'It will have to be something of surpassing interest to drag me from my research into subatomic cultures. What have you done, my friend? Robbed a bank?'

Rather uncertain how to take the man Ed said quietly, 'It's not me at all. I'm worrying over one Ralph Marshall, a friend of mine. He's in a hospital for supposed lunacy. He mentioned you just before they took him away. But actually he's no more insane than you are.'

'I am indebted for the compliment. Ralph Marshall, you say? Not 'Stinker' Marshall who nearly blew me up in the college lab, and who's now working on the Atlantic Shaft?'

'The same — only he isn't working any more. This is serious, Dr. Lloyd, really it is . . . ' Ed went on to relate the full details. Then he finished earnestly, 'You've got influence. You're an expert in optics, medicine, and all the rest. You know more than all those darned sawbones put together. And since you know a thing or two about crime too you might be able to discover if there is a special reason, other than a medical one, for detaining Ralph.'

'Frankly, Mr. Rutter, I am not a police officer. My stature is against it. As to Ralph, the situation is little short of preposterous!'

'I thought a true scientist never called anything preposterous! I really believe Ralph can see a city or something that we can't. I thought he had a neurosis at first. Now I know differently . . . '

'Hm!' Lloyd flattened his J on his brow again. He stood thinking.

'The firm will back up whatever measures you see fit to take,' Ed went on earnestly. 'If you can prove to medical satisfaction that Ralph is perfectly sane you will at least get him out of imprisonment. At least you should do so. If you can't, then maybe you can find the right legal means. Ralph has got to be released. He's a master engineer, and valuable.'

'I suppose you are aware that despite my brilliant reputation I am not at all in favour with the regular doctors, specialists, and patchers of human framework generally?' Lloyd asked calmly. 'My methods are unorthodox. At times, surprisingly enough, I have been called mad. My chemical work, leading me to deal in Latin so much, has led me to call many a man worse than a fool in a language he does not understand.

'I may, for instance, know optics inside out, but I am not a registered optician. However, the law entitles you to call in a specialist if you wish — and though not registered I am certainly a specialist. For two reasons — A, my regard for old 'Stinker' Marshall, and — B, my desire to see a proper engineer finish the Atlantic Shaft, I will look into the business. *Experto crede*, my friend — trust one who has had experience.'

'Quite,' Ed nodded, uncertainly.

'I have another reason — C,' Lloyd went on in his rumbling voice. 'If Ralph has somehow gotten his vision bent into another line of light waves he can be of invaluable assistance to science generally through his revelations. I'll see him.

'First, however, I shall have to prepare. Instruments are needed to try a case like this, and I shall have to bring influence to bear to get permission to make the examination. I'll advise you when I'm ready.'

Ed caught the small hand and shook it warmly. 'I can't begin to thank you enough for — '

'Then don't waste my time and your own,' the little scientist replied briefly. 'Good morning!'

★ ★ ★

It took a week, overcoming professional prejudice, for Brutus Lloyd to secure permission to examine. It was Ralph Marshall's firm, urged by Ed, who finally ordered it, and against that Flint could do nothing. Ed accompanied the diminutive, Latin-spouting scientist to the hospital in his small but powerful car and helped him to carry in a variety of instruments. There were moments when he felt inclined to smile at Lloyd's Derby hat, long overcoat, and neatly rolled umbrella. He had a remarkable gift for carrying that umbrella on his arm and thereafter apparently forgetting its presence.

Ralph Marshall was finally brought into the wide, light room singled out for the examination, and after a few words sat in the high backed chair. Dr. Flint and the summoned specialists, some of them smiling tolerantly, sat in a half circle round the instruments. Only Flint looked impatient, his fingers drumming on his bony knees.

Skipping round like a goblin in his overcoat, hat carefully laid on the surgical table, Lloyd first set up a curious object like a shimmering ball, connected to electrical devices on the tripod stand beneath it. It started to coruscate with startling radiance when the current was turned on. At times it filled the room with bewildering incandescence, then at others faded rapidly through the spectrum colours into invisibility. The spectators blinked. Flint stared hard.

Lloyd said in his rumbling voice, 'Did you see anything then, Ralph?'

'At the moment, sir, I'm looking at some — some sort of ball,' Ralph answered slowly. 'Solid looking piece of work. It comes and goes.'

'Hah!' Lloyd pressed a button with the ferrule of his umbrella. The ball seemed to vanish entirely, but Ralph became excited.

'Now it's quite distinct! It's hovering over the city streets!'

'Such rubbish!' Flint cried, leaping up. 'Dr. Lloyd, this is sheer absurdity!'

Lloyd surveyed him, eyelids drooping. '*Ex nihilo nihil fit* — from nothing nothing comes,' he observed. 'And I haven't finished yet, Flint. Sit down!'

Flint slowly obeyed, his lips a tight line.

'You and your tests!' the little scientist went on sourly; then he pushed his ball instrument to one side and proceeded to get to work with a needle-recording apparatus, shafts of crisscrossing light, and finally a prism device radiating all the colours of the rainbow.

'What did you see, Ralph?' he asked finally, stroking his J.

'I saw a ball, a prism, and something like a torch beam.'

'That,' Lloyd said, 'is exactly what I thought you'd see. You can relax for a moment. Now, gentlemen!' He spun round like a top and pointed his umbrella at the group in sudden accusation. 'Gentlemen,' he rumbled, 'I have pleasure in telling you that Ralph Marshall is not mad! On the contrary he is as sane as you are — saner probably. He is also one of the most useful acquisitions to science yet known.'

'Proven, of course, by this — this hardware of yours?' Flint asked sarcastically.

Lloyd was unabashed. His frosty blue eyes were bright with triumph.

'We all know — at least I know because I am a scientist of the first order — that the human eye is only capable of seeing within the ranges encompassed between ultra violet and infra red at opposite ends of the spectrum scale. Also there are sixty octaves of light, of which we see only one! Only *one*, gentlemen!' Lloyd raised his umbrella aloft dramatically. 'This ball instrument of mine is designed to cover the whole range of invisible light fields. By altering its light-reflecting capacity it gives off either the light waves *we* see, or the light waves beyond our range. In the latter instance it becomes invisible to us — but it becomes visible to Mr. Marshall! In other words, his vision has slipped into an octave higher than our own. So slender a margin, gentlemen — so unusual for it to happen. This is the first real case I have encountered. The other three instruments verified, prismatically, that he is indeed looking into a plane an octave above normal visual range.'

'From which,' Flint asked with deadly calm, 'you deduce what?'

'I deduce — A, that people move and have their being in this other plane; and that — B, an accident caused Mr. Marshall's vision to be warped into that plane.'

Flint snapped, 'Then these people are all around us? These — others?'

'Naturally!' Lloyd stood challengingly erect.

'Then in that case,' Flint said, smiling maliciously, 'you infer that these people occupy the same space as we do? That their city is superimposed over New York? Even you should know that no two bodies can occupy the same space at the same time.'

Lloyd's fingers quivered down his J of hair. Only the slightly higher pitch of his voice revealed his exasperation.

'*Nemo me impune lacessit* — no one affronts me with impunity,' he breathed. 'Your ignorance surpasses my highest expectations! Any expert physicist will confirm the fact that our space is only one of *thousands* of spaces! A molecule is made up of empty space in much the same fashion as the universe is mainly empty space. It is highly probable that the apparently empty spaces are filled with other matter working at a different pitch of vibration and therefore completely invisible to us.

'Matter dovetails and interlocks and each section is at a pitch of vibration which makes it invisible to its immediate neighbour. Nature has so designed her so-called empty space that other molecules move about it in the apparent emptiness — hence the belief of Mr. Marshall that he walks through buildings and that people walk through him!'

'Fictional nonsense, Dr. Lloyd,' Flint commented sourly. 'We are only concerned with facts. In my opinion Mr. Marshall is still completely blind and a victim of mental perturbations. I think I speak for my colleagues, too . . . ?' He glanced round sharply and there was a solemn nodding of heads.

'In other words,' Lloyd said slowly, 'you do not *want* to believe?'

'I didn't say that — '

'But *I do*!' Lloyd bellowed, thumping his umbrella on the floor. 'The whole lot of you — you in particular, Flint — are either a collection of conservative, unimaginative boneheads, or else you prefer to believe the dementia theory for your own purposes. Don't interrupt me, Flint!

You have the authority here, certainly. What you say goes in this hospital, and you might possibly scare other men into obeying you. But you don't scare me. I am Brutus Lloyd! I cannot legally force you into releasing Marshall — but I can, and will, do other things.'

'Such as?' Flint inquired calmly.

Lloyd put his Derby back on his head. '*Cadit quaestio* — discussion is at an end. Let's go, Mr. Rutter . . . I'll be seeing you again, Ralph.'

Lloyd gathered up some of his instruments and departed. Ed looked after him, then back at Flint.

'Listen, doctor, you're not taking Ralph back into imprisonment without plenty of opposition!' he snapped. 'I'm warning you — '

'Take it easy, Ed,' Ralph himself broke in quietly, rising from the chair. 'Causing a scene won't do any good.'

'Evidently the patient has more sense than anybody,' Flint observed dryly. He stood watching, lips compressed, as the male nurses came forward.

'I'll wait and see what happens,' Ralph

went on. He shook Ed's hand firmly and Ed concealed the surprise he felt as a hard lump of paper was pressed in his palm. What could Ralph be up to?

When he left the hospital a few moments later with the rest of the instruments he found Lloyd waiting for him in the car. Slipping in beside him he unfolded the crumpled note and the pair of them read in mounting surprise.

It was badly written, since Marshall had been unable to see the writing, but it was decipherable nonetheless:

'*Don't endanger anything, Eddie. I've been waiting for a chance to give you this note. I have discovered something almost incredible since this side-slipped vision came upon me. It is to my advantage that you let me stay in my cell for the time being. I have one or two things to look into. I think, but cannot yet be sure, that I have happened on a particularly amazing plot in this 'other world' which affects ours! And unless I am entirely mistaken Dr. Talford Flint is mixed up in it somewhere.*

'This possibly accounts for his fanatical desire to keep me under lock and key. Once I'm sure of my ground I'll pass on the news to you. See me visitors' day. If you can find out anything about Flint in the meantime all the better . . .'

Ed glanced up at Lloyd's thoughtful face. 'Well?' Ed asked briefly.

Lloyd did not reply; he only smiled as he started up the car's engine. But his face was preoccupied as he drove through the busy streets.

★　★　★

Ralph Marshall had made no idle observation in his note. His cell — for it was little better than that despite its furnishings — unknown to anybody else, was so placed that in the 'other plane' it overlaid a small, compact laboratory, in which a solitary, white-garbed scientist seemed to spend nearly fifteen hours of every day.

Invariably, Marshall saw him arrive as

soon as it was light; and he remained until about midnight. In the daytime he seemed to spend his time testing medical apparatus, peering into highly efficient microscopes, making notes watching queer animalcules slithering and twisting nauseatingly in glass test tubes.

Certainly Ralph did not like the man's face. It was cast in a ruthless mould. The lips were thin and tight, the jaw hard and cruel. The eyes, too, had the brittle brightness of a man driven by ambition to the exclusion of all finer sentiments. There were times when he seemed pleased to watch a queer, unknown animal — probably the equivalent of a terrestrial guinea pig — twisting in near-death under the influence of some mystic fluid he had injected into it. Apparently he was working in secret for nobody ever came to see him and he prepared all his own meals.

But above all things it was the notes he made so assiduously that interested Ralph. By walking the length of his cell he was able to look over the scientist's shoulder and read what was being put down. So far, his knowledge of the language was limited, but there were parts of it he understood, and in particular one name which was bound to be the same in any language — Flint.

Was it referring to the chief of this very hospital? That was what Ralph wanted to find out: it was his one reason for submitting so tamely to captivity. What connection had Flint — if it was the same man — with this trap-jawed scientist of another plane of existence, so close, and yet so infinitely far away?

Most puzzling of all to Ralph were the evenings. He would watch the Unknown sit for nearly two hours in a chair, motionless, his head tilted back on two leather pads like those adorning a dentist's chair. As he sat, his hand was at work on a neighboring scratchpad, making all manner of notes, mainly chemical symbols in which Ralph was not in the least versed.

It did not, however, take much deduction to discover that the daytime laboratory work was based on the evening time notes — but why did the Unknown have to sit like that? Ralph cudgeled his brains over it for many days but he got no solution. As a matter of fact, it was Ed Rutter who worked on that particular mystery.

Determined on his own account to more fully confirm Ralph's vague suspicions of Flint, he entered the hospital grounds by night — once Lloyd had discovered by various surreptitious methods exactly what part of the hospital the doctor occupied in his private moments — climbed the railings, and slid softly past the great isolation wards to the doctors' chambers' wing to the east of the hospital. To him it was not a difficult feat to climb to the balcony: his work in the Shaft had made him an adept climber.

He spent some little time discovering which window belonged to Dr. Flint's room, traced it finally from the rough sketch Lloyd had drawn. His hopes were verified when Flint came into the room, switched on the light, and without drawing the shades sat down at his desk to write.

Ed smiled grimly, withdrew from his

pocket a tiny, flat microphone, which Lloyd had given him. It went easily under the door-size window leading out onto the balcony. The rest of the instrument, hung around Ed's neck like a medallion, began to record whatever the microphone picked up.

Ed switched on the button and waited, listening to the small-size earphone. He heard nothing beyond the scratching of a pen. After a couple of minutes he tensed when a man came into the room beyond.

He recognized him as one of the doctors who seemed to be Flint's right-hand man. After closing the door and locking it he came over to the desk.

'Not too late, am I?' he asked briefly. 'I had that operation to finish on old Saunders.'

'No, Dutton.' Flint tossed aside his pen. 'I haven't started yet . . . '

'How long do you think it will be before we're ready?'

'Depends. Perhaps a week. There's little time to lose now. And besides I want to get everything perfectly arranged before this guy Marshall happens to discover the

41

truth. It's not likely that he will while locked in that cell — but if any fluke law can be brought along to release him he might discover plenty. Only by having freedom could he possibly come across Maravok's laboratory — and even at that only chance could lead him there. Just the same I've warned Maravok that we have a fellow with us whose eyes are geared to his particular space. He told me he was working on a visionary detector by which he'll be instantly warned if alien eyes discover him. Clever man, Maravok . . . ' Flint's voice was full of grudging praise.

Outside, Ed stood listening tensely, frowning in wonderment. On his chest the medallion-sized instrument was recording every word.

'About this fellow Lloyd,' Dutton mused. 'He's damnably quiet, isn't he? In face of all he said he'd do? Think he's up to something?'

Flint laughed harshly. 'Not him! The man's a clown — the biggest clown in New York City. He thinks he's a detective, a scientist, and God knows what all rolled into one. Five feet of empty boasting, my friend, and a lot of phony instruments to back him up . . . '

'Phony enough to prove that Marshall *was* and is looking into the plane you contacted,' Dutton pointed out uneasily.

'Well — yes,' Flint admitted. 'Rather a good thing he did find that out for it enabled us to know that Marshall's eyes *are* geared to the plane I've contacted. I suspected it might be so when Rutter called us to have a look at him in the first place. Most amazing case, Dutton. Yet, deeply though it stirs my professional curiosity, I cannot admit the truth of it with so much at stake. He must be kept out of the way, until we're ready anyway. Then it doesn't matter what he does!'

'Suppose Lloyd does manage to find a legal excuse for extracting Marshall? I don't think he's such a mug as he pretends to be.'

'That,' Flint said, 'is a risk we have to take. We've got to stall for time until I have every detail. If the worst comes to the worst we can always arrange an — er — alteration of diet for Mr. Marshall which will make him too ill to be moved.

We dare not kill him off: that would involve too searching an inquiry.'

In the brief silence that followed Ed controlled a fierce impulse to kick the glass window through, open the door, and dash into the room. He wanted to beat the living daylights out of the callous hospital chief. Only the realization of the necessity for subtlety kept him in check.

Presently Flint spoke again. 'Well, time's up!'

Ed peered cautiously through the window as silence dropped. Flint was seated in the armchair, head lying back on the cushion, hands resting lightly on the chair arms. He was gazing into space straight in front of him. Dutton was sitting opposite to him with a notebook and pencil, waiting.

'Now!' Flint exclaimed suddenly; then he started to talk in a quiet, monotonous voice. '*Having thoroughly impregnated the fluid, drop the cultures into it. There will be rapid metabolism. Then —* '

The monologue veered into the profoundest technique possible and could only interest a medical expert. But the thought of cultures and fluids, that certain sinister suggestion of a deep medical experiment, remained uncomfortably in Ed's brain. He waited for an hour until Flint had obviously finished, then he withdrew the microphone gently, climbed back over the balcony, and departed. This was definitely getting into deep waters, and only one man could swim in them — Brutus Lloyd.

3

Bacilli-X

The morning after Ed's activities Dr. Lloyd turned up at the hospital during the usual visiting hours. A nurse creaking with starch led him down the white enameled corridor to Ralph's room and admitted him.

'Ten minutes,' she proclaimed curtly, and locked the door behind her as she departed.

Ralph rose at the familiar bass voice, shook the small hand warmly.

'I've discovered something — ' he started to say, but the scientist cut him short.

'*You* have discovered something! Ralph, you don't know what a discovery is. Leave that to me! I will admit — A, that your friend Ed Rutter was helpful, and — B, that I might not have thought of the idea otherwise. But my genius provided the instruments . . . Listen!'

Lloyd went into a complete recounting of Ed's adventures the previous night, slapping the table with his umbrella for emphasis.

'*Fervet opus* — the work goes on busily,' he finished in triumph.

'Seems to me,' Ralph said slowly, 'that there's only one explanation. This guy who you say is called Maravok, does exactly the same thing as Flint. He sits back and rests his head as Flint apparently does . . . Oh, I forgot. You don't know all the details about the laboratory, I can see. It's like this . . . '

'Telepathy!' Lloyd announced when the story was over.

'Yes; telepathy. I was going to say that. There is no barrier to thought reaching into this other plane, is there?'

'None whatever. In fact we contact these planes in the normal way. We have all had the feeling of being watched in an empty room, or that 'I have been here before' sensation. I should say a trained telepathist might get into touch with other planes around us. More of us might see these planes if our eyes were as cockeyed as yours. But what is Flint *driving* at?' The umbrella stubbed the floor impatiently. 'So far as I can make out from the record he made Flint is constantly taking down details of a medical experiment devised by this guy Maravok.'

'Just the same as Maravok is taking details from Flint,' Ralph puzzled. 'It's an exchange of information. See here!' Ralph pulled his scratchpad from his pocket. 'You take this and see if you can understand what it's all about. Most of it is in medical terms; stuff I've taken down from looking over Maravok's shoulder. Not very well written, I know, but maybe you can figure out something. His figuring seems to be perfectly similar to ours and some of the terms may make sense to you. You know most things in medicine . . . '

'*All* things in medicine,' Lloyd corrected modestly, thrusting the pad in his pocket. 'More I see of this the less I like it,' he went on. 'This fellow Flint is the least angelic person I've ever met.

Telepathy, medical experiments, cultures, and so forth, when practised by him spell something sinister. However, maybe I'll find out something from these notes. I'll be back again next visitor's day and tell you how I've got on — also to learn anything you may have found out.'

Ralph nodded. The door lock clicked as the nurse returned.

'I forgot to tell you,' Lloyd said, as he turned to go. 'Ed sent his regards, or his love, or something . . . He's at work and couldn't make it. Ought to be his own master, like me. Much better! Well — *nil desperandum* . . . '

Lloyd met no official as he passed down the corridor, looking like an underpaid clerk. Though there was no law against his presence in the hospital he preferred if possible to avoid a direct contact with Dr. Flint. And he managed it successfully.

Half an hour later he was in his laboratory, perched like a gnome on a toadstool before his desk, poring over the scrawled notes of Ralph, then listening to the playback from the recording Ed had made. The more he pondered over them the grimmer his resolute little face became. Certain technical terms leapt readily to his mind, and where they were in a different language the interpretation, from the formula itself, left little doubt as to the actual meaning.

For two hours Brutus Lloyd brooded stroking his J of hair at intervals. Thus Ed Rutter found him during the lunch hour when he slipped in to inquire as to any progress that had been made.

'Anything fresh?' he asked quickly. 'You saw Ralph?'

'Sure I saw him . . . ' Lloyd slid from his stool and paced the laboratory slowly, hands deep in his smock pockets. Then looking up sharply he said, 'I believe we've happened on something unimaginably big! We — or at any rate Ralph — have unearthed a medical plot which for sheer villainy beats anything I ever heard of! So far as I can make out this person Maravok is about as ruthless in his ideas as Flint himself. Both of them are — A, exchanging medical information; B, Flint is telling Maravok how to nurture cholera germs which are apparently unknown in this other space, and against which there is no protection; and — C, in return, Flint is finding out from Maravok how to cultivate a bacilli which will cause paralysis and death when introduced into the human system! It is a bacillus entirely unknown to us, and Flint would be able to start something as virulent as the Black Death!'

Ed's eyes opened wider. 'Hell, we *have* found something!'

'*I* have found something,' Lloyd averred, his eyelids drooping insolently.

'Well anyway, it's been found. But listen, why should two men telepathically exchange secrets concerning plagues in their respective lands? It isn't even sense . . . '

'*Corruptio optimi pessima* — the corruption of the best is worst,' Lloyd sighed. 'Two clever men pawning genius for gross material gains. Look at the situation and what do we find? A — Flint is head of the hospital. B, he is in a fixed position that any qualified medico could take over. C, a Plague hits the country. An unknown, smashing Plague! What then? Suppose he — Flint — were the only man with an antidote? And he *has* an antidote; I'm convinced of that . . . The demand for his services would be colossal. His antidote, or serum, would net him millions of dollars. He, and whoever else is in on the job — there will be others I'm sure — would reap a fortune. You see? A deadly plan with human lives as the means to an end. Since Flint can probably cure all those who are impregnated he probably considers it is quite a safe move and not a murder risk. It's clever, though I'm loath to admit it. Damned clever!'

'Of course we tell the police?' Ed demanded.

'And tell them Ralph Marshall saw most of this in another plane of space?' Lloyd asked. 'You overrate the imagination of the law, my friend. I could explain it to my friend Inspector Branson, but without solid proof even he might become a trifle annoyed. No, I intend to nurture the bacilli for myself first and find out their potentialities. If they turn out as

I expect I shall hand the results to the police chemists to satisfy themselves. As for Flint, his recorded voice is enough to convict him. But we must be *sure*! I must also know exactly what his past history has been.'

'I'd help you if I could,' Ed said, rather anxiously. 'As it is I'm tied up during the day, but I could go to the hospital again by night and try to — '

'Emphatically no!' Lloyd slapped his tiny hand on the bench. 'You did it once and got away with it; next time you might not be so lucky. Anyway, I have all I need for evidence. If Flint gets wind of our plans it will put Ralph in a spot. Just leave things as they are and rely on me. Now get out. I've work to do.'

Lloyd completed his medical experiments during the afternoon. In the evening Ed Rutter found himself gazing through the microscope upon twirling, squirming life-forms of minute size drifting through thick fluid.

Lloyd gave a rather harsh laugh. 'Bacilli-X,' he commented grimly, handling the slide with care as he returned the culture to the glass phial. 'There's enough in this tube to reduce the population of New York to paralysis. The devils multiply like hell . . . '

'What's next?' Ed asked briefly.

'Next we track down Flint's history from the medical records . . . ' Lloyd locked the culture phial away in the safe securely, then scrambled into his vast overcoat. He nodded toward the door.

They began with the library and studied Flint's career from *Who's Who*. His career had been distinguished anyway. He had degrees without number, but it was the nature of his various published works that gave an insight as to the real man. In three years he had published *Crime and Medicine*, *Possibilities of Thought Transference*, *Telepathy*, *Mind and Inter-Space*, *Criminal Action and Reaction*, and *The Psychology of Crime*.

Lloyd, satisfied, headed for the nearest booksellers before they closed and managed to buy every one of the books enumerated. Then he returned home.

Without a word, an overlong pipe crackling in his mouth, he settled down to read. Ed started to read too because there was nothing else he could do. But he had no idea of what the diminutive scientist was looking for.

As a matter of fact Lloyd read for three consecutive nights, probably the days too for all Ed knew to the contrary, before he seemed to arrive at a conclusion. On the third evening, shutting the last of the volumes with characteristic abruptness, he said:

'My conclusions are verified! Flint besides being a brilliant doctor is also a master-telepathist. He either has a mind ideally suited for transmission and reception of thought, or else he has learned the art better than any other man living in this world. Either way he has communicated with this other plane.

'But it is also clear that he has definite leanings towards a criminal state of mind. Like many men with too much scientific and medical knowledge he doesn't know where to stop. Not all of them have that spark of divine genius that makes them invaluable to the world. That is left to the few.'

Lloyd licked his lips at the personal reflection and went on. 'Though not actually possessing a police record, Flint certainly has been — and still is no doubt — in close contact with many underworld dives. He could not otherwise have written these remarkably clear treatises on the relationship between crime and medicine. He refers to several specialized types of criminals, whom he has obviously met. He gives fictitious names, of course. I fancy it might be possible, however, to track down the various people mentioned in these volumes by way of police department records. Tomorrow I'll see what Inspector Branson has to say about it. I'm ready to move now.'

'But what do you hope to gain by tracking down these criminals?' Ed demanded. 'It's Flint we want — not the subjects of his treatises.'

Lloyd smiled tolerantly. 'How do you imagine a Plague would begin, my friend? Do you think Flint would walk about sticking hypos into people? He would have agents scattered everywhere. What better place is there to recruit them than from the ranks of crime with which he is already in contact?'

'Funny! I never thought of that!'

'*Quandoque bonus dormitat Rutterus!*' Lloyd murmured. 'Even the worthy Rutter sleeps at times. Fortunately, I remain awake.'

★   ★   ★

Inspector Branson was cordial, but doubtful, when Lloyd tackled him in his office at headquarters the following morning. Ed, on a day's vacation to see the thing through, added his own corroboration. Not that Brutus Lloyd needed corroboration: he had it in the voice record and culture phial.

'Have this tested by your chemists and they'll find something they never knew about before which can paralyze the population of New York,' Lloyd announced, holding the phial up. 'Then have them check the formula by the voice record Ed Rutter here took. That can't damage your infernal red tape surely?'

Branson took the phial and laid it down gingerly. He looked at the little scientist thoughtfully, then finally he nodded.

'All right, Lloyd, I'll do that much. Frankly, though, I never quite know how to take you. You get the most extraordinary scientific ideas sometimes and — '

'And they are always right,' Lloyd finished calmly. 'This is no exception. However, I am not a detective — in the sense of snooping after criminals, I mean. I am a scientist. That is why I have to enlist your aid in tracing the living originals of the descriptions given in these books by Flint. You'll find them blue-penciled. You can manage that?'

'Don't see why not.' Branson flipped the pages. 'Take about a couple of hours. Suppose we manage it? What then?'

Lloyd picked up his umbrella. 'I'll tell you in a couple of hours. Meantime some lunch is indicated. Let's go, Ed.'

They returned at the appointed time to find Branson ready with a pile of record cards.

'Ten of 'em we've easily identified from

description and surroundings,' he announced. 'The rest aren't so easy. These ten are always under police observation, anyway.'

'You could rope them in for questioning?' Lloyd inquired.

'Nothing easier.'

'Then go to it. You'll find one of them will crack wide open and admit he's in contact with Flint. If one of them does that the rest is easy. You can round up the others in no time — if it's necessary. It's probable that Flint hasn't started circulating his bacilli, yet, and I don't suppose these crooks will know the real issue anyway.'

'I hope,' Branson said, pressing a button on his desk, 'you're all straight about this, Lloyd. After all, basing your original theory on a man who can see into another space is a bit tall even for you.'

'*Ab uno disce omnes*, Branson,' Lloyd responded, beaming. 'From a single case infer the whole.'

'You'd better be right,' Branson observed grimly.

Lloyd stroked his J pensively. 'I'm sitting right here until those crooks are roped in, if I have to wait a week. Once you're satisfied, Branson, a warrant for Flint's arrest can follow pronto.'

4

Scientist of Another World

Ralph Marshall wondered more than once what Ed and Lloyd were doing as the days slipped by. At least he had complete confidence in them, which was everything. For his own part he did not relax his efforts in the slightest: in fact he could not do so very well since he was obliged to look into the laboratory of Maravok every time he took his glasses off.

As on the other occasions, Maravok spent each night doing his telepathic work and making notes. During the daytime he made medical experiments and also put the finishing touches to a device like a metronome. On the fourth night he had the 'metronome' finished, stood watching it pensively.

Ralph moved across his cell, the better to see what was going on. He stood

61

gazing at the inverted pendulum as it swung rhythmically to and fro — but it struck him as curious that when he moved towards it — actually across his own cell of course — the pendulum ticked all the faster and increased its swinging to nearly double.

A sense of unexpected danger touched him. He saw Maravok's cruel face set in granite lines. He turned sharply, gazed unseeingly at Ralph and then round the laboratory. Ralph backed away instinctively and the metronome resumed its former leisurely beat. He felt — he knew — that that device was somehow geared to register alien vision in the laboratory. In truth it was the device of which Maravok had already spoken telepathically to Flint.

Ralph sat down to watch, clenching and unclenching his fists. He saw Maravok settle in his chair and lie back to concentrate. As he remained motionless various thoughts twirled through Ralph's brain. He knew quite well by this time that the scientist was planning something pretty diabolical from a medical stand-point, something that was no doubt destined to endanger his own people as much as Flint's scheme would endanger the people of the everyday world.

But how was it possible to get at the man from another space? Unless, perhaps, the metronome . . . ? That, so far, was the only thing Ralph had seen which was capable of reacting between planes. Probably it was accomplished by the vibration of bodily aura passing between molecular spaces. That was quite a logical possibility, anyway. If so . . .

Ralph looked at the instrument again. It was not fastened down in any way. The shelf on which it stood was directly over an array of bottles of fragile glass containing all manner of chemicals. Some of them were probably explosive if mixed together. Certainly there were numerous acids.

Ralph began to smile to himself grimly. Perhaps there *was* a way to destroy this other-world laboratory and Maravok with it. Back of Ralph's mind was the remembrance of the alarm clock on the mantelshelf in the living room at home — the thing that had slid itself along by its own vibration every time it had rung. Suppose that the metronome could be made to vibrate strongly enough to slide over the edge of the shelf? It might, if he went close enough, and Maravok was sitting with his eyes closed, concentrating.

Ralph rose up and walked across the cell slowly, watching the instrument immediately increase its rate of pendulum swing. Closer — and it still increased. He reached out both his hands and waved them in the space where he imagined the thing must be. That action, as the electricity from his body passed across the gap, made the pendulum become a mist. The instrument, even as he had hoped, began to tremble and slide uneasily along the shelf towards the edge.

At that moment Maravok opened his eyes and looked up. He catapulted out of his chair, arm outthrust, but he was a shade too late. The metronome slipped into the midst of the glass bottles below, and in his frantic urgency Maravok missed catching it completely.

Ralph stood watching the results of his handiwork — but he did not watch for long. The acid jars spilled their fuming contents into saline looking chemicals. There was a sudden unholy spurt of flame and deep yellow smoke. Almost instantly it was followed by a blinding flash of incandescent light. No noise, not a sound, but the glare and vibration hurled Ralph back across the cell as though he had been thrown. His eyes twinged and stabbed as though rammed with white-hot needles. He could not see the laboratory any more, only a spotted curtain of chaotic dark.

Gasping with pain, clawing at his eyes, he scrambled to his feet. He had hardly done so before the door lock clicked and somebody came in.

'Who's there?' he demanded sharply, staring into the dark.

'Just me, Mr. Marshall.' It was the unmistakable voice of Flint. 'I thought perhaps a little chat might be advantageous. You see, I only just learned this evening how completely I have played into your hands. I realize that you know of my telepathic activities with Maravok, whom you killed only a moment or two ago by some method or other . . . '

Ralph stood rigid, his pain abating. He tried to place the position of the voice. It was by the door. He clenched his fists and said nothing.

'Tonight Maravok learned for the first time that there were other eyes watching,' Flint went on. 'His instrument revealed it. It could only be you. Since you must obviously know most of my plans I cannot imagine anything better than for you to be the first victim of the plague that is about to strike the continent. I have everything ready. My agents will be advised. Right here in my hand is a hypodermic, one injection from which will insure your death within fifteen minutes. Since countless others will be affected within a few hours, and since only I possess the antidote, it will obviously not be a case of murder but death from an unknown disease. Simple, isn't it? Had I known you knew so much I might have done it sooner — '

'Damn you!' Ralph roared suddenly, and charged for where he knew the table was. He seized it, slammed it forward to the position of the doorway, blundered round it. Flint gasped with pain, then his voice came again, thick with fury.

'You can't get out of here, Marshall! Not with those warped eyes of yours! You're as blind as a bat, and I know it! You can't get out, I tell you — '

Ralph clawed suddenly at the door handle, then he stopped at a grip on his arm. Instantly he whirled up his fist into the dark and felt it impact bone. Flint went staggering back across the room, tripped, and dropped his length, the syringe flying out of his hand.

Ralph's sharp ears heard it tinkle on the woodwork round the carpet, and that was enough for him. He plunged forward until he stumbled over Flint. Seizing his neck he raised him, hammered home his right fist time and time again into the doctor's face . . . until a sudden smashing blow in the jaw stopped him for a moment.

He lashed out again, missed, and another blow hit him in the face. It was followed by one over the head that laid him flat on the floor. He felt his senses reeling. A weird miscellany of noises came to him. The sound of running feet, the desperate breathing of Flint and the scratching of his hands as he clawed for the syringe —

Then for Ralph the sounds faded away into silence.

★ ★ ★

Ralph returned to consciousness to the knowledge of a throbbing head and a bandage across his eyes once again. He stirred slowly and the voices of Ed Rutter and Dr. Lloyd reached him simultaneously.

'Take it easy, Ralph; you're O.K.,' Ed said. 'But we were only just in time.'

'In — in time? How? Why?'

'Thanks to me the police came to arrest Flint,' Lloyd said modestly, after briefly recounting the earlier events. 'We couldn't find him in his study, but nurses had seen him going toward your room. So we followed. We got him just before he could sink a hypo into you.'

Ralph relaxed with a sigh. 'Then that's

settled! I cleaned up Maravok and you cleaned up Flint!'

'What!' Lloyd cried. 'You mean you did something to cause Maravok to be destroyed?'

'Sure I did . . . ' Ralph related the full facts. At the end of it Lloyd drew a deep breath.

'This explains much!' he exclaimed. 'I had a look at your eyes when you were unconscious and my tests showed they were almost normal. Something had shifted them out of that other plane to the normal one, but even my wide experience could not imagine what it could be. I thought it might have been the result of the blow Flint gave you when he hit you with a chair. Now I know the truth. The blast of flame in that other plane gave the necessary optical shock to slam your vision right back to normal after a brief spell of blindness, which you are now undergoing. In two days' time you'll be seeing as well as ever again.'

'You mean it?' Ralph cried eagerly, sitting up again.

Lloyd glanced at Ed and smiled. 'Ralph

does not know it,' he observed gravely, 'but *stat magni nominis umbra* . . . He stands in the shadow of a mighty name . . . And the owner of that name never makes mistakes.'

The little scientist was right. Two weeks later Ralph was back on his Shaft.

2

THE MURDERED
SAVANTS

1

Vision of the dead

'Another scientist murdered! Extry! Extry! Paper, sir?'

'Yeah.' Rex Thomas took the evening edition of the *Observer* and studied it with a frown — indeed, more than a frown. There was a look of blank horror on his young, good-looking face.

Dr. Brian Thomas, famous metallurgist, Rex Thomas' own brother!

'It isn't true,' Thomas whispered to himself, stupefied. Then he went on, thinking aloud,

'A knife in his heart like all the others before him? No — it's too damnably horrible!'

And he was the fourth scientist in a row! Four prominent scientists in as many months —

Horley, the great neurologist had been slain first. In quick succession had followed Bennet of physics, Jansen of astronomy and now —

He looked up sharply, controlling himself as he became aware of people on the sidewalk glancing at him curiously. With sudden decision he thrust the paper in his pocket and headed swiftly for police headquarters.

Inspector Branson, the bull-necked chief of the neighbourhood precinct station, looked up from his desk as Thomas was shown into his office.

'Inspector, I — I just read about the murder of Dr. Brian Thomas. He was my brother, my twin brother. I'm Rex Thomas, radio specialist.'

Branson smiled faintly. 'I'm aware of that, Mr. Thomas. Matter of fact, you've saved us the trouble of roping you in for questioning.'

'Roping me in — ?' Rex Thomas echoed in amazement.

'We're satisfied with your actions,' Branson said reassuringly. 'At the time of the murder, you were working overtime at the Apex Radio Factory — last night, that is. Don't worry; we know all about you.

'We wanted to question you about your brother's associates. Do you know any of them? If we can get a clue to anybody who might have a reason for getting him out of the way, we might have a lead that will direct us to an arrest. Can you recall anybody likely to have a motive for wishing your brother out of the way?'

Thomas scratched his blond head.

'Guess not,' he sighed. 'I came here to ask if you'd got any line on the killing — though I don't suppose you would tell me if you had. I rarely saw my brother. He lived in a world of his own — a scientific world of research. I have my life; he had his. All I know is that he lived in a house in the suburbs with one manservant. I can't imagine who'd want to kill him.'

'Hmm.' Branson compressed his lips. 'Just as we can't yet see why this steady murdering of scientific men is going on. No apparent motive. It's the damnedest thing I ever heard of!'

'A maniac, perhaps?' Thomas suggested, thinking hard.

'Perhaps — However, while you're here

you can add your identification to the body. It's in the morgue.' Branson pressed a button. 'After you have identified the body, you are free to go, but not out of the city. You'll probably be needed later on. Everybody connected with your brother is under suspicion at the moment.'

'I understand.' Rex Thomas nodded; then as the plainclothes man came in he turned and left in his company.

At the morgue he went through the ordeal without a word, merely nodding his head dazedly as he gazed on the waxen face of his dead twin — a face so like his own.

He hardly recalled how he went out into the street again. Though he had had few dealings with his ambitious, scientific brother, the murder had come as a considerable shock. Thomas went home to his apartment lost in thought. He was just in time to catch the telephone ringing noisily.

'Yes?' he said absently into the mouthpiece.

'Hello, Rex!' It was the familiar voice of

Beryl, his fiancée. 'I rang before but I got no answer.'

'No — no, I'm late.' Thomas roused himself. 'I've been at police headquarters.'

'That's what I'm calling about. I've just seen the paper. It's terrible, Rex! Terrible! What are you going to do? What are the police going to do?'

'I dunno. I've got to stay in town, that's all 1 know. But I don't think I'll have much trouble — my alibi is watertight.'

Thomas forced himself to realities, put more warmth in his voice.

'Thanks for the sympathy, Beryl — thanks a lot!'

'But of course I had to sympathize!' she cried. Then, quietly, 'But I admit I had another reason too. Are you fit to come to the dinner tomorrow night? You know, the one dad is throwing? It's a pretty highbrow affair, I suppose, but there'll be lots of ignorant folks there, like you and me, who aren't interested in scientific mumbo-jumbo. After what's happened I wondered if you'd be fit to — '

'I'll come,' Thomas said briefly. 'Don't

worry, I'll be okay. I've yet to see the event that makes me pass up an evening with you. See you tomorrow evening, dear.'

'Around seven. Goodbye.'

' 'Bye, Beryl.'

Thomas hung up slowly, then shook himself.

'This won't do, Rex, m'lad! Snap out of it! Grab yourself a shower, a bite and some shut-eye. Then you'll be all set.'

He followed out his own prescription accurately — but when it came to sleeping, he hit hard against a problem. The moment he started to doze something happened to him. It was as though he were dreaming while still awake.

A vision, hazy in outline but nonetheless distinguishable, insisted on hammering itself into his consciousness. He could have understood a strong recurrent reminder of his radio work, for he had been working until all hours on a new receiving set design for weeks — but this was something utterly different.

The scene represented some sort of laboratory, or else a surgery. It seemed to be filled with chemical and medical apparatus, electronic tubes, magnets, mazes of wire. In the centre of the room was a long surgical table, obviously for the purpose of major operations, if the arc lights, at present extinguished, hanging overhead were any guide.

But easily the most puzzling thing of all was the presence of six chairs, like those used by a dentist, with helmets on the top of each. Curious helmets, indeed, like those of an aviator's outfit. On a rack nearby, shielded by glass screens, were numberless probes, scalpels, and saws . . .

Thomas woke up sweating, cramped his eyes shut, then opened them again. Convinced he was the victim of a nightmare, he tried to settle himself again. But the vision came back, in a slightly changed form. For a brief moment or so he saw his brother — his *dead* brother — lying on the formerly empty surgical table, gazing in sheer terror at something unknown.

Straps were about the other's body, pinning him down. His head had been shaven as bald as a peeled egg. He seemed to be saying something, struggling to speak.

'Brian!' Rex Thomas screamed suddenly, sitting up. *'Brian!'*

He was shuddering all over. Shakily he switched on the bed light and gazed around the quiet, deserted room. Nothing was any different.

The events of the day, of course! The horrible things that had happened had all warped into his consciousness and produced this. It had to be a dream, because his brother was dead . . .

He waited a long time to calm himself, and thereafter slept at fitful intervals with visions here and there. He felt pretty washed out by the time he rose next morning. And sown deep in his mind was a profound bewilderment.

Many a time in the past his being a twin had given him unexpected visions of his brother, particularly in time of trouble — but how could it apply to this occasion when his brother was in the morgue?

A bad dream — nothing more.

★   ★   ★

Rex Thomas arrived to attend Beryl's dinner party after a day of gradual recovery from his heavy night. The immense sweep of the girl's home — the residence of Jonathan Clayton, famous inventor — the myriad lights, the efficient servants, the cordial voices, did much to clear Thomas' mind. And the girl herself, an entrancing dark-haired, grey-eyed vision in evening dress, practically consummated the cure.

'Hello there, Rex!' Beryl came forward eagerly as he entered the great lounge and picked his way among the guests. 'How's tricks?'

She smiled at him impishly, then seeing his serious face she went on,

'Anything wrong, dearest? You look tired — Your brother, of course?'

'Yes — sort of preying on my mind.' He shrugged his shoulders. 'But I swore I'd leave my troubles at the front door, and I intend to.'

Someone else was greeting him then.

'Glad to see you, Rex.' It was the girl's father who came up with extended hand. Big, grey-headed, strong-necked, he looked more like a champion athlete than an inventor — and probably the best inventor the United States Government had ever employed for regular service.

'Evening, sir.' Thomas returned the grip. 'You seem to have quite a few people around here tonight. I — '

'Indeed, yes! Come along, I want you to meet some of them. See you later, Beryl.'

The girl nodded slowly, her face clearly disappointed at the sudden separation. But her father was determined. One by one Thomas found himself being introduced to some of the country's leading scientific experts. Among them were the thin-faced, unpleasantly sharp Professor Eliman, wizard of brain surgery; and then a gnome-like little man under five feet in height, with an immense forehead down which curled a lock of hair shaped in a Napoleonic 'J'.

This little man was talking in a surprisingly bass voice to Joseph Clough, the financier, when Jonathan Clayton tapped him on the shoulder.

'Lloyd — a moment. I want you to

meet my prospective son-in-law. Rex, meet Dr. Brutus Lloyd. You can call him an expert in any branch of science and criminology, and be right every time.'

'Correct,' Lloyd beamed, extending his small hand. Then, his frosty blue eyes narrowing a little, he added,

'Clayton errs, my young friend. He should have said prospective *step* son-in-law. Eh, Clayton?'

Clayton shrugged. 'I regard Beryl as my own daughter.'

'*Culpa levis* — excusable negligence,' Lloyd sighed. 'Unfortunately my profession demands an accuracy of facts — even to daughters. If either of you think the less of me for the correction, it won't make the least difference.'

Clayton said nothing. Rex Thomas gave a faintly puzzled smile, the smile of a man who hears the unexpected for the first time.

Then he said, 'I seem to have heard of you before, Dr. Lloyd.'

'*Seem* to!' Lloyd echoed, glaring. 'Before you, young man, you behold the greatest scientist of the day — *teres atque*

83

rotundus, a man polished and complete.'

'Don't mind him, Rex,' Clayton chuckled. 'He got that way from reading Latin in his chemistry experiments, and — '

'Of course,' Lloyd said, changing the subject, 'you're the brother of the late Brian Thomas?'

'Yes, and there's something I'd like to — '

Thomas broke off as Beryl came up in high spirits.

'So here you are, Rex! Dad, what do you mean dragging him off like this to meet your brain-bulging cronies? We've things to talk about.'

Thomas found himself whirled away, but for the life of him he could not find the inspiration necessary to rise to the intended jollity of the occasion.

'Sorry, Beryl,' he apologized, as the girl went in to dinner on his arm. 'I've a heck of a lot of things on my mind. Tell me something — your last name isn't really Clayton, is it? Dr. Lloyd let the cat out of the bag.'

Beryl shrugged. 'I never thought it mattered. After all, you're going to change my name anyway, so why worry?'

'I'm not worrying,' Thomas said. 'You're all that counts, anyway. Incidentally, is Dr. Lloyd here professionally or as a guest?'

'Guest, of course. He's known dad quite a long time. Why?'

'Just wondered if he could explain something rather queer. It'll do later.'

The girl glanced at him curiously, but said nothing. For some reason she spoke little during the dinner; and Thomas for his part ate little. He was aware of feeling rather out of the conversation, which seemed to shuttle back and forth between financial expositions on the part of Joseph Clough and scientific comments by hatchet-faced Professor Eliman.

Dr. Lloyd seemed to have little to say, but Thomas noticed his shrewd little eyes darting from one face to the other as he dug heartily into the well-prepared courses.

Rex Thomas felt thankful when the meal was over. Quietly he took Beryl to one side.

'I'm going to borrow Dr. Lloyd for a while. Mind?'

She sighed. 'Seems I've little choice. You're sure *I* can't help you? I'm good at patching up troubles.'

'You'd fail this time. See you later darling.'

Thomas caught Dr. Lloyd in the hall as he was crossing with Jonathan Clayton to the lounge.

'Oh, doctor, a moment! I wonder would you mind very much if I consulted you?'

The little scientist halted and frowned. 'I have hours for work and for play, Mr. Thomas. While appreciating your desire to utilize my vast powers, I must say — '

'But this is urgent!' Thomas cried. 'Desperately urgent!'

'Well — ' Lloyd stroked his 'J' of hair pensively. 'All right,' he agreed.

'Take the library,' Clayton invited, throwing open the door for them. 'See you later.'

2

The Stained Scalpels

'Now,' Dr. Lloyd snapped, as the door closed, 'I have little time for trifles, Mr. Thomas. Please come to the point immediately.'

'Fair enough. It's about my brother, Brian. He was murdered like three other great scientists before him, and nobody knows why, the police least of all.'

'Hah!' Lloyd snorted, his small face cynical.

'He was murdered,' Rex Thomas went on tensely, 'and yet last night I had the strangest dream. In fact, it wasn't a dream — more a kind of vision. In that vision my brother was still alive, yet only a few hours before I had seen him in the morgue.'

Lloyd gestured irritably. 'I am not here to play games, Mr. Thomas. What is this? A new insight into nightmares, or what? I have no time for half a story. *Qui timide rogat docet negare,* young man — he who asks timidly courts denial! Be frank. I, Brutus Lloyd, order it.'

'Sorry, sir. I thought — ' Thomas shrugged, puzzled by the scientist's odd manner.

'You see,' he went on, 'it struck me as strange that I should get a vision like that with Brian dead. We were twins and — well, twins often get visions of each other doing things. Common between them. Sort of telepathic link, you know.'

Lloyd's eyelids lowered insolently. 'I require no tutor in scientific matters, Mr. Thomas. However, the statement is interesting and — A, twinship with a dead body is intriguing, and — B, the problem of the recent murders has commanded my attention. So — continue!'

Thomas obeyed, and during the narrative Lloyd sat perched like a gnome on the edge of the desk, stroking his lock of hair thoughtfully. When it was over he raised an eyebrow.

'A laboratory, eh? Helmets? Dentist's chairs? Hm-m! You are quite sure it was your brother's body in the morgue?'

'But of course! I'd not be likely to mistake my own twin, would I?'

'Twinship of minds — twinship of motives,' Lloyd mused. 'Hm-m — most interesting.'

'Again,' Rex Thomas said slowly, 'I'm wondering if the murders will stop now. Suppose Dr. Clayton happened to be the next one.'

'If he did, grief would descend on Beryl, eh?' Lloyd asked dryly. 'You want me to clear all this up in order to save your fiancée from distress.'

'Partly that, yes,' Thomas admitted. 'It will take a detective of your ability to get to the bottom of the whole thing.'

Lloyd rose in scorn. 'Detective!' he sneered. 'I, sir, am a specialist! I do not work for gold, but for pleasure. God gave me a brain beyond the normal, and I use it. If, of course, the Government should reward me afterward — Well, *exitus acta probat* — the result justifies the deed.'

'You mean you'll look into it?'

'For three reasons,' Dr. Lloyd responded. 'A — I must find out for the sake of my psychology notes how a dead man can impress a living twin; B, I must find out why an unknown laboratory has chairs like those in a dentist's surgery, and C,' — he smiled blandly — 'the mightiest of brains needs relaxation. This case will provide it.'

'I don't think so,' Thomas said nervously.

'What you think is mere foolishness, young man. Have you enough pull to get yourself a brief vacation?'

'I guess so.'

'Excellent! I shall need you probably for physical aid; I am no Hercules. Mentally I am more than sufficient. You will be at my house at exactly nine tomorrow morning. And now, *redire ad nuces* — let us return to the 'nuts',' Dr. Lloyd punned.

He opened the door and marched briskly to rejoin the guests.

★ ★ ★

It was late in the evening when most of the dancing and fun were over that a knotty point of argument arose among the scientists. It led them finally, Rex Thomas and Brutus Lloyd included, into Jonathan Clayton's own private laboratory.

'Here you are then, gentlemen — synthetic flesh!' Clayton cried triumphantly. 'Does this convince you or not?'

He raised something that looked like pink rubber from a bowl and stretched it back and forth.

'The latest miracle for surgical work,' he added quietly. 'Practically as good as the real thing, full of minute fibres to carry the bloodstream. Doubt it if you can!'

'You see, it doesn't do to doubt the mind of Dr. Clayton,' observed Professor Eliman, smiling cynically. 'I've known about this invention for some time, only it wasn't ethical to reveal it without permission.'

'And I'm grateful for your confidence,' Clayton said seriously. 'This is not a Government invention; I can use it privately and aid medical science immensely. I had hoped to create life — '

'Waste of time, in my opinion,' Joseph Clough commented. 'I made my money soaking people, not helping them. However — '

'I suppose,' Lloyd remarked, 'you financed this synthetic flesh idea, Clough?'

'Sure. I've financed dozens of Clayton's private inventions. Plenty in 'em, on the side.'

'*Auri sacra fames* — accursed lust for gold,' Lloyd sighed. Then as the scientists gathered round to inspect the synthetic flesh, he wandered slowly around the laboratory, his keen eyes glancing up and down. Presently he stopped at a horizontal mirror lying directly under a massive telescopic tube.

The mirror was rather surprising. It was not polished and clear, but of unusual construction.

'My latest,' Clayton said proudly, hurrying up. 'Not quite ready yet for offering to the astronomical field. It's an element detector.'

'Can it be that I, who know all things scientific, am at a loss?' Lloyd mused, frowning.

'Probably, this time. This is a new idea. Watch!'

Clayton moved to a switchboard and busied himself with controls. The laboratory roof rolled open along a section to a clear moonlit sky. Upon the mirror there appeared the moon's image, but instead of the usual craters and seas there was a multitude of network colours of every imaginable hue.

'The moon,' Clayton observed. 'Ordinarily it is revealed as a white surface, of course. Only a tiny fraction of that surface has been excavated by the handful of astronauts who have reached it. What minerals and ores it may possess are unknown — or were unknown until I invented this.

'It is a well-known fact that different metals give off different light-values, ordinarily undetectable. But this instrument of mine, by a prismatic system, can detect different light-values by reflection instead of actual illumination.'

'Clear as mud,' one of the scientists laughed.

'I'll make it clearer,' Clayton apologized. 'We know the elements of any star by the flame colour we get through the prisms. Reflected light has defeated us so far — but I've solved it. Hence the reflection of light from the moon reveals clearly what elements it has.

'See,' — he pointed his finger at a dull grey streak — 'here is lead. Probably a great field of solidified lava. In turn, we have iron ore deposits, gold seams in considerable quantity, silver, oxides — '

'Remarkable!' Lloyd exclaimed, his eyes brightening. 'A satellite worth a good deal, eh?'

'Definitely,' Clayton smiled, switching off. 'A world of valued metals revealed for the first time through my invention — but unhappily a world two hundred and forty thousand miles off. We have space travel, of course — but the chemical rockets employed are astronomically expensive — no pun intended! Using existing rockets, it would actually cost more to get to the moon to mine them, than the metals themselves would sell for!'

'I've suggested ways and means of developing a new — and economical — way of crossing space — in fact, most of us here have — but our host won't listen,' Professor Eliman said. 'Sometimes I think you're unprogressive, Clayton. A genius, and yet too conservative. You say that economical space travel would lead to war and conflict — a twenty-first century gold-rush!'

'I do,' Clayton sighed. 'That is one reason why I am rather reluctant to reveal the secret of this detector to any but my immediate friends. When men realize what is up there, in the sky — '

'And there are other dangers,' Thomas put in quietly. 'A maniac is at work somewhere killing off brilliant scientists. Suppose you were singled out, once your profound knowledge became known?'

'Absurd!' exclaimed professor Eliman, with a cynical grin. 'The maniacal killings of scientists are not worth considering. At least, *I* am not afraid, and I'm sure Clayton is not.'

' 'Course he isn't!' exclaimed Joseph Clough reassuringly.

'I just happened to recall my brother's murder, that's all,' Thomas said quietly.

Clayton gave a shrug. 'Isn't this getting

rather depressing, gentlemen?' he asked. 'Suppose we repair to the lounge.'

Lloyd marked time with the group until Rex Thomas caught up with him.

'This is not the laboratory you saw in your vision, I suppose?' he asked softly, as they went through the doorway.

'No. And in any case I wouldn't distrust Dr. Clayton. I know him too well.'

'Many of the dead scientists were his friends,' Lloyd murmured. '*Fide, sed cui, vide*, Mr. Thomas — trust, but see whom you are trusting.'

'You don't think — ' Rex Thomas stared, appalled; but Lloyd only gave an unfathomable smile and gently massaged his 'J' of hair.

★   ★   ★

When Rex Thomas arrived at Dr. Brutus Lloyd's suburban house next morning, he found the little scientist ready and waiting in his open roadster outside the gates. If anything, Lloyd's big Derby hat and enormous overcoat made him look odder than ever.

'About time!' he snapped testily. 'Get in!' Then as he started the car moving he added, 'We're going to see Inspector Branson. He has the matter in hand. Good man, Branson — within limits.'

'So I thought.'

'Your opinions do not concern me, Mr. Thomas. Tell me, did you have any more visions last night?'

'Well, sort of. I saw that unknown laboratory rather hazily, but not my brother.'

'Yet if you saw the visions and they are directly connected with your brother, it seems to indicate he is still alive,' Lloyd mused. 'In other words, *mens invicta manet* — the mind remains unconquered.'

'Yeah — something's damned phony somewhere and I don't like it.'

Lloyd said nothing further, seemingly lost in thought until police headquarters was reached. Then he marched into Inspector Branson's office holding his crook-handled, neatly rolled up umbrella.

'Morning, Branson. Four scientists have been murdered — all with knives. What have you done about it?'

'I — '

'Nothing!' Lloyd thumped his umbrella on the floor. 'Just nothing! And for this we pay a sales tax, a property tax, and Heaven only knows what else!'

'So,' Branson said bitterly, 'you've decided to bust in with some high-flown scientific theories, eh?'

'There is no law against a specialist, Branson — and such a specialist! You ought to be grateful. *Brute ad portas* — Brutus is at the gates!'

Branson gave a resigned sigh. 'Okay, I know it's useless to try and get rid of you. Matter of fact, this scientist business has rather got me stymied anyway.'

'Ah!' Lloyd's eyes glittered with approval.

'So few clues — in fact, none at all,' Branson growled. 'In each case, the murder was committed in a room which has a gravel path outside it — so there were no soil footprints or anything else to guide us. No finger marks on the knives or anywhere else.'

'And each time the murderer drove the knife straight to the heart?' Lloyd asked slowly.

'Straight to the heart,' Branson affirmed.

'Hm-m. The paper mentioned surgical knives. I'd rather like to see them.'

'Right.' Branson pressed a button and gave instructions to the clerk who entered. 'I think they're called scalpels,' he added.

'You think! *Vis inertiae*!'

'Huh?'

'The power of inertness,' Lloyd beamed, snuggling back in his chair. 'Of course, I admit that genius is only given to the few — '

Then he straightened up again as the clerk returned with a steel box. Branson laid out the ticketed and labelled knives on the desk with his handkerchief.

'Exhibits One to Four,' he commented briefly.

The diminutive scientist studied each one in turn, narrowed his eyes at the tarnished stain on the gleaming blade in each case.

'Scalpels, yes,' he said slowly. 'But the stains?'

'Blood, according to the laboratory. The scalpels are leading us to look for a surgeon as the culprit. And — '

'Blood tarnishing stainless steel?' Lloyd asked pointedly. '*Da locum meliorbus*, my friend — give place to your betters! Blood!' he sneered. 'Clear those bone-heads out of your laboratory and get some real men of science. This isn't bloodstain: it's an acid of some kind — and it's on each knife, too.'

'But I have the report — ' Branson began, but Lloyd waved a small hand.

'Light your pipe with it! Don't presume to talk to me of science, Branson.'

He pondered a moment, then wrapped one of the knives up in his handkerchief and thrust it in his pocket.

'I'm taking this — and don't start any arguments. I want it for two reasons — A, to prove what the stain really is; and — B, to prove to a very dense world that it is not always the obvious solution which is the right one.'

'In other words, you aim to make a monkey out of me?' Branson snapped.

Lloyd chuckled as he headed for the door, remarking dryly to his puzzled client,

'*Avito viret honore*, Mr. Thomas — he flourishes on ancestral honours. You'll hear from me later, Branson.'

'I'd better!' Branson roared, as the door dosed. 'You're stealing my evidence!'

3

The Dead Undead

'It is possible,' Dr. Brutus Lloyd said, as he drove down the street, 'that — A, your visions were *not* the result of supper; and that — B, your brother Brian is not dead, or at least was not dead when you saw him in your vision.

'It is likewise possible that — C, extreme fear caused telepathic power to be established between you. That is by no means uncommon in twins.'

'But I saw Brian in the morgue! You forget that!'

'I forget nothing!' Lloyd retorted. 'Nothing!'

He became silent after that, patting the knife in his pocket reflectively now and again. Once he arrived home, he stalked straight into his laboratory, threw on a gigantic smock, then went to work on the knife with reagents and burners. Thomas,

102

interested but baffled, lounged around watching.

At last the little scientist straightened up and fondled his lock of hair.

'Bloodstains! Bah!' he exploded finally. 'The stain on this knife contains proportions of sodium chloride — salt, to the uneducated; phosphate, lime, a trace of sulphuric acid, and cochineal for coloring. No man with that mixture in his veins could ever live. No man — not even I, and I can do most things.'

'Then where did the stains come from?'

Lloyd said slowly, 'The facts are these: A — the knives were found in the heart each time; B, they were removed by the police, and the blades would not be contaminated with anything else afterward, that much is certain; and — C, they contain the fluid which was in the bodies at the time. That is obvious.'

'Then why didn't the police chemists find the mistake?'

'They probably did — they must have, but they couldn't reconcile the mystery, so they said it was bloodstain. You understand?'

Rex Thomas scratched his head. 'Damned if I do! Sounds nutty to me.'

'Branson referred to accurate stabbing by the murderer each time,' Lloyd mused. 'We are asked to believe that the murderer was able to drive true to the heart on *four distinct occasions*. I don't believe it!'

'Then just what do you believe?'

'I believe that the bodies were never alive anyway!'

'*What!*'

Lloyd grinned insolently at the sensation he had created. He added calmly,

'Synthesis, my friend! Synthetic flesh!'

'But, dammit it all — ' Thomas gave a gasp. 'Say, Dr. Clayton is the one who understands synthesis. But it is inconceivable that — '

'*Palmam qui meruit ferat*, Mr. Thomas — let him bear the palm who has deserved it. Yes, he invented synthesis, *but* — What I do not like are — A, the sinister implications behind all this; B — the suggestion of its being a cover-up for something else; and — C, the decided shadow cast across Clayton.'

For a long time Dr. Lloyd stood brooding over the knife in his rubber-gloved hand; then turning suddenly he picked up the telephone, quickly contacted the police headquarters.

'Hello, there! This Branson? Good! This is your superior, Brutus Lloyd. I want you to exhume all four murdered men right away. They never lived, anyway — '

The receiver squawked in response and Lloyd stood glaring at the instrument.

'What do you mean, am I mad?' he snorted. 'You're talking to Brutus Lloyd, Branson — *clarum et venerabile nomen* — an illustrious and venerable name! I am a scientist; you are not. Therein lies infinity — You *what*? Why, man, I believe the four scientists never died by a dagger but were actually used for some other and probably more diabolical purpose.'

Again the receiver rattled with Branson's irate voice.

'My reasons?' Lloyd asked calmly. 'A — the blood on the knives might be a mixture worth selling to a chemical works; B — no murderer could strike

105

dead true to the heart four times on the run, and — C, most significant of all, the scientists who are presumed dead would probably be far more useful alive.

'Dig up those corpses! What? Oh, I'll bring the knife with me tonight. See you at seven, and you'd better have a body dug up. No reason to? The Brian Thomas death hasn't been looked into yet? Then conduct your autopsy on him. See you at seven.'

Lloyd put the receiver back, and as he did so Rex Thomas added,

'Of course, Brian won't be buried yet. His immediate associates have planned a big funeral. I heard about it this morning. I asked to go, of course — tomorrow. Only you wanted me, you said, and — '

'I fancy that the events of this evening will make the undertakers short of a job,' Lloyd murmured. Then more brightly, 'But now for lunch, my friend. This afternoon my brain will knit into a concrete whole what it has already learned; and this evening — Well, *flectere si nequeo superos Acheronta movebo*

— if I cannot move the Gods, I will stir up hell! Come!'

* * *

On the stroke of seven, Dr. Brutus Lloyd's goblin-like figure walked into Inspector Branson's office. The inspector was looking rather bewildered but he was cordial enough.

'You were right,' he said, as Lloyd returned the knife to the desk with a clatter. 'Come and see the result of the autopsy. Only been at work on the so-called Brian Thomas so far, but the other bodies are probably the same — '

'Definitely!' Lloyd thumped his umbrella down. 'Don't dare to doubt it!'

He and Thomas followed the inspector to the surgery down the corridor, and presently stood gazing at the result of the medico's work under the bright lights.

It was the corpse of Brian Thomas that lay there — and when he could bring himself to look fully at it, for the medical mutilation had rather sickened him, Rex Thomas experienced dumb wonder. For it was not a real man that lay there — but a contrivance of springs and padding which gave the illusion of stiffness and yet fleshy pliability! A partly metallic skeleton simulated the weight of a real body. The rigor mortis of a dead body was perfectly simulated.

The staggering fact was that the 'man' was only a model with a flesh covering. There were no internal organs, not even a heart. The wound from the assassin's scalpel had simply passed through the outer casing.

'This — this is incredible,' Thomas whispered. 'So like my brother; even to the eyes.'

'Dead eyes always remind me of dusty grapes,' Lloyd murmured. 'These eyes probably belong to a wall-eyed dog. They give the impression of death.'

'As to the identity of appearance to the real Brian Thomas, any expert modeller could do it with synthetic flesh as easily as with clay, if he had the frame to work on,' Branson said thoughtfully.

'Which reminds me — I've got some

new information. Crandal, the well-known sculptor, has disappeared. Been missing for several months now. His relatives thought he had gone to South America, but they seem to think now that something must have happened to him. They asked us to help only this afternoon. Seems to me it might mean something.'

'There are times when I realize why you became an inspector,' Lloyd commented cynically. 'Crandal, eh?' he repeated sharply. 'Hm — I seem to recall a lot of his big sculpture shows were financed by Joseph Clough. Mystery, indeed! *Crescit eundo* — it increases as it goes.'

'This synthetic flesh is a new one on me,' Branson muttered, shaking his head. 'And as to the reason for such elaborate precautions — I give up.'

'Without an autopsy, you would have considered this and the other three bodies to be normal corpses,' Lloyd observed. 'Proof indeed that my genius is far ahead of the normal intellect.' He pushed his Derby farther back on his scholarly brow and said gravely,

'Branson, we face a crisis!'

'So I've figured for some time,' Branson said sourly.

'Consider the facts! We have — A, somebody with a knowledge of synthesis and sculpture; B, such a person must be a brilliant scientist, and — C, when four famous scientists are picked out *by* a scientist, it is for a reason distinctly detrimental to the victims and the world at large. Otherwise, *why* the precautions?'

Lloyd paused, then added, 'Suppose, Branson, that you had found synthesis. Impossible, I know, but suppose you had? Suppose you could model a man at will but could not make him live. What would you do?'

'Open a waxworks, maybe,' Branson hazarded, rubbing his jaw.

'Or else make imitation corpses, fix daggers all ready in their apparent hearts, and steal the real people!'

'Hell! You've got something there. But one couldn't model a person so accurately without knowing every detail of his physique.'

'Most of that could be overcome by photography,' Lloyd snapped. 'And cameras can fit into a tie pin if necessary. Personal contact would help, of course; therefore we can assume that the culprit knew each of the dead scientists very well indeed. Well enough to know every anatomical detail worth knowing — '

'The culprit's a doctor; got to be,' Branson said doggedly. 'Those scalpels prove it! Seems to me the thing to do is to check up on the immediate acquaintances of the four dead scientists and start a new trail from there. Eh?'

Lloyd smiled blandly. 'Commendable — but do you imagine so clever a criminal as this one seems to be would appear as *himself* each time when near his intended victims, just to provide you with a clue? *Satis eloquentiae, sapientiae parum*, Branson — eloquence enough, but so little wisdom!'

'Then we'll look for somebody who knows something about synthesis!' Branson retorted.

'That's easy,' growled Rex Thomas. 'Dr. Clayton invented it.'

111

Lloyd put a hand to his eyes and thumped his umbrella on the floor.

'*Deus avertat!*' he groaned. 'God forbid! He has to go and throw away my most important clue like that — Idiot!' he blazed, waving his umbrella overhead. 'Why the heck don't you keep your trap shut?'

Branson smiled bitterly. 'Keeping things back, eh, Lloyd?' he asked coldly. 'Trying to steal a march again with your cockeyed science? Okay, we'll see! I'll have Dr. Clayton roped in on suspicion of murder in two bats of an eyelash. Why, the thing's a cinch!'

'Wait!' the little scientist roared, his blue eyes frigid with command. 'Wait, confound you! I'll not have you upsetting my well-laid plans! I wasn't trying to hold back anything. Why should I? I can outthink you any time. No, I wanted to piece together one or two things first.'

'Yeah? Such as?'

'A — would Clayton freely admit his knowledge of synthesis if he were connected with an affair like this? B — what is the connection between

Clayton and his wife?'

'Wife?' Branson stared. 'I thought she was dead.'

'No. I found out long ago that his wife, the mother of Beryl, is serving a life sentence in a State penitentiary. Her name before marrying Clayton was Kimberley. Beryl is the stepdaughter of Dr. Clayton, of course.'

'So what? What's all this got to do with synthesis?'

Lloyd sighed. '*Brevis esse laboro, obscurus fio* — in labouring to be brief I become obscure. Not that I expected you to see anything in the observation anyway,' he added tartly. 'You — '

'Oh, the hell with all this!' Branson interrupted impatiently. 'I've got to pin a conviction on somebody, and Dr. Clayton is that one man.'

'Now wait a minute!' Lloyd snapped. 'Get this, Branson. I'm not obstructing you in your duty, but I have certain privileges I mean to exercise. I can't stop you clapping a warrant on Clayton — but I want two clear hours in which to see Clayton first. In taking him out of the

113

way, you may ruin the best clue I've got. Now, what about it?'

Branson hesitated. 'Well, all right. I guess that can't make much difference — but I warn you, it'll be too bad for you if you mess things up!'

'If *I* mess things up!' Lloyd smiled insolently; then, thumping his Derby back into position on his head he moved to the door. '*Festina lente*, Branson — make haste slowly. Come, Mr. Thomas.'

Out in the corridor Rex Thomas came out with a string of apologies. The only response he got was a flinty glare from Dr. Lloyd's blue eyes.

'Well, I'm sorry anyway,' Thomas repeated, as they settled in the car. 'But just what do you figure you can get out of Dr. Clayton?'

'A solution,' Lloyd snapped. 'Now keep quiet. I must think.'

He started up the engine with a sudden roar. Soon the car left the comparatively quiet main street, headed through the heart of the city, then out to the night-swathed country road leading to the scientist's suburban residence.

'Listen, sir,' Thomas said presently, 'what do you make of all this? For instance, I didn't know Beryl's mother was in prison. What's that angle?'

'There isn't any. At any rate, not yet. I put it in to give that fool Branson something to work over. Pity about Branson — he's got brains, only they're muscle bound.'

'Well, about my brother? Do you think he's still alive?'

'Possibly — ' Lloyd was silent for a while then unburdened himself again.

'Let us consider. A — the four scientists have been kidnapped and models of their bodies left in their places to present the impression of murder. B — their deaths would set the police looking for a murderer and *not* a kidnapper. C — we also realize that the kidnapper knew he could not return the bodies, hence the synthetic duplicates.

'Therefore, surely your uneducated brain can grasp that something fiendish is indicated which will incapacitate said scientists from any chance of return!'

'Good Lord — yes!'

'*Ah! Interdum vulgus rectum videt* — sometimes even the rabble see things aright. The kidnapper would have no reason to take the scientists if he intended to kill them. He could do that without leaving models. And what are scientists noted for?'

Lloyd preened himself for a moment in his own ego.

'For their *brains*, young man! Their brains!'

'You don't mean they have been kidnapped so something can be done with their knowledge?'

'Exactly! In that vision of yours you saw a surgery and your brother with a shaven head. Heads are shaved before brain operations — '

Lloyd's small face was set into granite lines now.

'*Graviora manent*, my young friend — the worst is yet to come. The man who made the synthetic bodies is a first-class modeller — and we may assume the disappearance of Crandal, the sculptor has something to do with that. A first-class surgeon would be needed for the synthesis. And that — '

Dr. Lloyd broke off and glanced in the rear-view mirror as the roaring of a powerful car became evident behind them. Rex Thomas twisted round in his seat and was met with a dazzling blaze of headlamps.

'Doing sixty, I'd say,' he cried. 'If he's not careful — Hey, what the devil — '

He fell back in his seat and stared ahead in wild alarm at the narrow road. Almost at that moment an immense sedan swept alongside and suddenly drove inward.

Lloyd's small hands missed the steering wheel of his roadster entirely. The car twisted sideward, careened over the bank, then went smashing helplessly through a mass of scrub and dust to the base of a deep ditch. It brought up with a crash on its side.

Head singing from the impact, Thomas eased his position and listened for a moment. For the time all was quiet — then at a sudden flash and crackle of flame from the engine Thomas came to life.

'Dr. Lloyd!' he yelled. 'Hey, where are you — '

'Here!' the scientist panted, struggling to free himself. He became visible against the rapidly gaining flame, his Derby jammed down onto his nose.

'My foot — Give me a tug, dammit! Can't see where I am — '

Thomas fell out onto the grass, caught the little scientist round the waist and heaved with all his strength. They both fell clear as the ignited gasoline spurted and crackled over the remainder of the car.

With a sudden effort Lloyd tore his hat free, stood glaring at the flaming wreck and stabbing his still safe umbrella fiercely in the ground.

'Deliberate!' he breathed, his bass voice quivering. 'Now we know there is something definite. Scum! *Servum pecus*! Servile herd! That car cost me plenty — However, the insurance is paid up.'

'We're losing time,' Thomas told him anxiously. 'Whoever was in that car was heading Clayton's way. Incidentally' — he frowned — 'I got the number just before we went over the bank. What was it now — XJ 4782.'

Lloyd looked vaguely surprised. 'So, there are times when another brain can be quicker than my own. Remarkable! Now stop drivelling and help me up the bank. Swine! They'll pay for this!'

At the top of the bank Lloyd stared grimly down the dark road.

'About four miles further yet to the Clayton place,' Thomas said.

'I am quite aware of it. Come on.'

As they trudged Thomas said, 'Wonder how they knew it was us in your car?'

'You mean me!' Lloyd retorted. 'You don't count, Mr. Thomas. The enemy has nothing to fear from you, whereas they stand appalled at my genius. Seeing you, the brother of the missing Brian Thomas, and me in close company for several days — for I do not doubt we have been surreptitiously watched — and finally seeing us emerge from police headquarters and head this way, it would be sufficient for the dumbest criminal to grasp that we threatened danger.

'We were singled out for destruction by

'accident'. Plenty will probably happen now.'

'You're right. We'd better hurry — '

'I am not a track-runner — nor have I legs like an ostrich. *Ultra posse nemo obligatur* — none is obliged to do more than he can.'

After that they trudged on wearily in silence, for something like forty-five minutes. Then they moved quickly to the side of the road as a fast car came speeding up from the distance with headlights blazing. To their surprise it stopped beside them and Inspector Branson's familiar voice came forth.

'Well, well, if it isn't Brutus himself! Out of gas? Or isn't that possible?' the inspector finished with malicious meaning.

Lloyd ignored the challenge. 'Where the devil are you going?'

'To the Clayton residence. Got a call from there a few minutes ago from the head servant or somebody. Old man Clayton's been stabbed and — '

'And you sit there making wise-cracks?' Lloyd roared. 'Get a move on, man!

Quick!' he bawled at the driver. 'Get in, Thomas — don't stand there gaping.'

The car shot forward again. Pinched beside Branson, Lloyd said briefly,

'They had the impudence to run me off the road. It was a black sedan, number XJ 4782. Send out a squad car to nab it, and you will also probably get the man we want — and Dr. Clayton.'

'But he's stabbed — '

'More model work, I fancy. Anyway, we'll soon find out.'

4

Ambition Diabolical

Once they got to the house and were shown into the library by a worried manservant, they found Beryl there alone, pacing nervously up and down and twisting a handkerchief in her hands. In a moment Rex Thomas ran from the group and clasped her in his arms.

'Okay, Beryl, take it easy,' he murmured. 'You're all right. We are all here now — '

'*I* am here,' Lloyd stated didactically, with a flourish of his umbrella. 'And I still pin you to your two-hour promise, Branson. I'm going to do the talking here.'

'That'll be a change, anyway,' Branson admitted sourly.

Lloyd's eyelids dropped cynically, then he swung to the girl.

'Now Miss Clayton — or rather Miss

Kimberley — where is the body?'

The girl looked at him in tearful surprise.

'But — but Dr. Lloyd, why so official? You usually call me 'Beryl' — '

'Where,' he repeated calmly, 'is the body? I am here as a specialist, not as a guest.'

'Do you have to be so damned blunt?' Thomas snapped.

'Yes. *Necessitas non habet mores* — necessity knows no manners. I — '

'Father's in — in the laboratory,' Beryl said quietly; then with a sudden hysteria,

'It's so horrible! Awful! Parker — that's the manservant — heard a crash in the laboratory and went in to investigate. It's terrible to think dad might have lain there all night otherwise.'

'And Parker phoned for the police?' Branson asked curtly.

'Of course. In fact, he had done it before I knew of the tragedy.'

Branson gave a sympathetic nod. For his part Lloyd turned briskly, and from familiarity with the house went straight through the hall and into the laboratory

123

— that same laboratory in which the gathering had taken place only the previous night.

Without pause, the scientist went to the sprawling figure lying face upward on the floor, knife buried in its heart.

The moment he held the dead wrist Lloyd gave a grin.

'More rubbish for the garbage can, Branson,' he announced briefly. 'Body's stone cold, even though it has been dead for supposedly only an hour or so. Synthetic, like the others.'

'W-what?' Beryl gasped in amazement, hanging onto Thomas' arm.

'A phony!' Lloyd said. 'See — ' And ignoring the girl's cry he yanked the knife out of the breast and drove the keen blade across the outflung hand. In response the first finger was sheared off clean. But it was as hollow as the finger of a glove.

'It's horrible! Horrible!' Beryl whispered, gazing.

'At least you might be more considerate in your stunts, Lloyd,' Thomas snapped, noting the girl's white face.

'Do not presume to dictate procedure

to me, Mr. Thomas!'

'What does it all mean?' the girl broke in urgently. 'Where is my stepfather?'

'Kidnapped,' Lloyd said briefly. 'Branson, have some of your men look the grounds over. There ought to be footprints this time.'

His keen eyes went round the laboratory and finally focused on the unlatched main window and an overturned instrument stand below it.

'Clumsy fools,' he murmured. 'That is what startled the manservant, obviously. That fallen stand. Had the body remained until morning, as was intended, its coldness would have seemed natural — Hm-m!'

'What?' Branson asked, as he saw Lloyd gazing at an instrument case. As the scientist made no answer, the inspector went over to him and looked upon the glittering array. Then Branson's brows knitted. Of ten scalpels, five of them were missing from their clips.

'Beryl,' Lloyd said, more familiar again, 'how often did Dr. Clayton practice surgery?'

'Not very often — except sometimes when Professor Eliman used to call and they made experiments together. Why?'

'Each of the knives that have been stuck in these four — or rather five — model bodies have come from here!' Branson retorted. 'That's why!'

'But — ' The girl looked mystified; then Lloyd said slowly,

'Since Dr. Clayton was not heard to call for help, it is possible that he was threatened with a gun by somebody at this window here. Hm-m — Beryl, your stepfather was the only inventor of synthetic flesh in this country, wasn't he? Or I should say, *isn't* he?'

'So he led us to believe, yes. But surely, Dr. Lloyd, you are not trying to suggest he made a model of himself, are you? That *he* is behind all this?'

Lloyd glanced at the instrument case and stroked his chin,

'No, I think he has proved himself innocent,' he said. 'Nor would he be likely to kidnap himself. That clear to you, Branson?'

'Well, yes — though I have known

criminals to apparently rub themselves out in order to make themselves appear one of the victims.'

'*Semel insanivimus omnes* — we have all been mad at some time,' the little scientist observed. Then with sudden decision,

'No — not Dr. Clayton. I've known him a long time and he's on the level. But somebody else, close to him, is *not!*'

'Well?' Branson waited expectantly, as Lloyd pulled his 'J' of hair resolutely and muttered to himself.

'*Quaestio vexata* — a vexed question. Give me time! A great brain hastens slowly — '

'Yeah, and while you're spouting Latin, Dr. Clayton is probably in danger of his life! That reminds me — I've got to send out a call for that squad car. Be back in a minute.'

Branson went out vigorously; and presently Lloyd said,

'Your father — stepfather — made no secret of his synthetic invention, Beryl; but he did suppress the formula, to the best of my information. That right — or did anybody else know the formula besides him?'

'Why, yes — practically all the scientists who came to see him — most of whom have been murdered since, or kidnapped.'

'Hm-m,' Lloyd mused. 'And to scientists synthetic flesh would appeal from the scientific and not the diabolic point of view. The only man closely acquainted with Dr. Clayton who is not a scientist is Joseph Clough.'

'The financier? Yes,' Beryl admitted. 'But aren't you forgetting that he helped to finance many of father's inventions?'

Lloyd gave a grim smile. '*Ubi mel, ibi apes* — where the honey is, there are the bees! I am just recalling that Joseph Clough also knows from this telescopic mirror here that there is gold on the moon — '

'Gold on the moon!' echoed Branson, coming in. 'What's going to happen next?' he demanded. 'Anyway, I've given that car number to headquarters; they'll put out a tracer for it. My boys tell me there are footprints about the grounds, all right — heavy ones, as though something

128

had been carried by the person whose feet made the impressions. And — '

'If you have quite finished — ' Lloyd said coldly. Then in the surprised silence he went on talking.

'Clough, from his long association with Dr. Clayton, must know all about synthesis, just as he knows the physical details of the other scientists he kidnapped. Don't you see? He knows from that mirror that there is gold on the moon — a vast fortune, if he can only *get* it!

'Gold is the one bait a man of finance would fall for, whereas a scientist would not.'

'Some day,' Branson said, 'I shall know what you are talking about. You mean Joseph Clough, the Wall Street big shot?'

'None other. My unerring judgment leaves no other conclusion.'

'Except the one that the critics are right when they call you nuts,' Branson commented. 'Anyway, where's the proof?' He waved his hands helplessly. 'What is all this about gold on the moon?'

Lloyd told him. The inspector nodded dubiously.

'Maybe, but that gold is an awful ways off.'

'Two hundred and forty thousand miles,' Lloyd stated calmly.

'And the only way to get there is by spaceship — and only the government has them! How do you figure any individual could get hold of a spaceship?'

'That,' Lloyd said, gazing around under drooping eyelids, 'is what puzzled Joseph Clough! So he kidnapped five of the best scientists to have them work it out! I recall a remark made in this laboratory last night, to the effect that Clayton had refrained from trying to invent a new, cheaper system of space travel for fear of possible after consequences.'

'And I remember something too,' Beryl put in, thinking. 'Sometime ago, though, Mr. Clough once asked father and some of his scientist friends if they would pool ideas and try and work out a way to get at the gold lying on the moon — that and the other valuable ores.

'They refused for the same reason as father — because it might invoke wars and crime. Besides, they were pretty sure they couldn't figure out a method — anyway, not individually.'

Branson murmured, 'They wouldn't do it of their own free will, so they may be having to do it by force.'

'Couldn't figure it out *individually*,' Lloyd breathed. 'But if it were done *collectively* — My God!' He stared blankly in front of him. 'If a surgeon were fiendish enough, he could — '

Lloyd swung around. 'If five of the greatest brains in the country were brought together to give a common result, there is no end to what might not be done! Science would leap ahead at terrific progress!'

'You mean mechanically pooled brains?' Rex Thomas asked slowly.

'Yes! You saw the operating theatre, didn't you? The fake bodies were stabbed with surgical knives, and they were taken from here with the obvious intention of deflecting guilt onto Dr. Clayton — until it came time for him to be taken as well.

'A — Joseph Clough is the money behind the enterprise; B — Crandal, the sculptor, has been 'appropriated' to make models; C — we are still short of a scientist to do the actual brain surgery, if any. Whom else but Professor Eliman, the renowned wizard of brain surgery? He, of all men, has avoided being attacked so far! Of course — because he is the culprit!'

'I believe you've got something there,' Thomas said. 'Remember how damned sure Eliman was last night that he wouldn't be overtaken like the rest of the scientists?'

'I've got to admit it, Lloyd, you know your surgeons,' Branson said reluctantly. 'Next thing we do is head for Eliman's place and rope him in for questioning.'

'No!' Lloyd shook his head adamantly.

'What d'ya mean, no?'

'Give me time to speak!' Lloyd retorted. 'Rushing to his home won't do any good — besides, you'd need a warrant anyway, or maybe you know that. Clough isn't the kind of mug to come because you ask him. What we need to know is all important — namely, the whereabouts of the laboratory where all the dirty work goes on!

'*Fons et origo malorum* — the source and origin of our miseries. There's one way to find out — make a phone call to Clough and play my hunch. If it's right, he'll unwittingly lead us to his laboratory.'

'We've a phone here — ' Beryl began, but Lloyd waved her aside.

'I shall phone within watching distance of his house. You stay here. There may be danger. Come, Branson!'

★　★　★

Twenty minutes later Dr. Lloyd was making his call. Branson crammed into the phone booth beside him with his ear to the outside of the receiver. Lloyd covered the mouthpiece with his handkerchief and raised the pitch of his rumbling voice a little.

After preliminaries with a servant Clough spoke.

'Well? Who is it?'

'Something's gone wrong,' Lloyd said briefly. 'Better get to the laboratory right away. I'll see you there.' Clough seemed to hesitate. 'If you mean that clown

133

Brutus Lloyd is on the track, don't let him worry you.'

Lloyd glared at the instrument and said gruffly,

'I can't explain any more now. Hurry up. It's urgent!'

He hung up and asked laconically, 'Well?'

'Guess your hunch was right. He's in it all right,' Branson admitted. 'Seems to have summed you up pretty well, too. Think he'll fall for the gag?'

'We'll soon know.'

They climbed back into the car, moved farther up the road and into a side street. Sure enough, a monstrous limousine drew up after a while outside the Clough residence and the financier himself came hurrying out. After a quick glance up and down he jumped into the car and it moved smoothly away.

'Follow it,' Branson snapped at the police driver. 'And don't be seen tailing it even if you have to kill your lights. Lose him and I'll kick you off the force!'

The driver did not lose his quarry, though it was difficult keeping track through main streets and intersections, but at last they drew clear of the city and finally struck a country road. At Branson's orders the police car lights went out. Far ahead the red light over the limousine's rear license plate had become stationary.

Lloyd stared out into the night with Branson beside him.

'Nothing there, except an old house or something with all the windows dark,' the inspector said.

'What did you expect — the Sphinx and the pyramids?' Lloyd asked sarcastically. 'Clough probably owns the property anyway. We may find plenty. Let's go — and have your revolvers ready!'

'What about you?' Branson asked ill-humouredly.

'My umbrella, man, my umbrella! Come on!'

They climbed out and sped swiftly in a wide detour across the dark field, presently came within range of tree-lined grounds. Thomas caught Lloyd's arm suddenly.

'Say — take a look! Two cars there

— one the black sedan that tried to run us down earlier, and the other is Dr. Clayton's! Say, they must have kidnapped him in his own car! What the hell — '

'Now I *know* I am a genius,' Lloyd breathed. 'Definitely!'

'When you've finished telling us you're a brainy guy, maybe you'll tell us what we do next?' Branson snapped acidly. 'Railings all around the place — '

'Then we climb over. After all, Branson, you said I made a monkey out of you — '

With surprising ease the little scientist set the example, mastered the high railing with ease and dropped down with his vast coat parachuting around him. In silence all of them gathered, then moved swiftly under the leaf-bare trees. Dimly across the drive they could see the parked unlighted bulk of Clough's now deserted limousine.

'What now?' Thomas whispered.

'Reach! Drop your guns!' snapped a heavy voice — and with a cracking of twigs and underbrush Joseph Clough came up in the starlight.

'*Drop them!*' he thundered, as there was brief hesitation.

'Better take it easy, Clough — ' Branson started saying, but the financier cut him short.

'Dr. Lloyd, you'll find a well three yards from where you are standing. Move to it, and descend into it. And don't get any original ideas!'

The little scientist said nothing. He moved forward slowly with arms and umbrella raised, finally found the well referred to. Clough flashed a torch onto well-cleaned steel footrests.

'Down — the lot of you!' he barked.

Devoid of weapons there was nothing else to do. The well ended in a short tunnel, obviously some long disused sewer from the house. At the end of the tunnel a door was half open, from which gushed white light, clearly electricity.

'Go on — into the laboratory,' Clough ordered.

The party obeyed, marched forward into the white-lit expanse. Another armed figure came quietly from behind the door and said briefly,

'You can lower your hands, but don't try anything.'

That voice seemed to smash the whole laborious investigation to pieces, for it was not the voice of Professor Eliman; not even the voice of Dr. Clayton.

It was the voice of Beryl!

Involuntarily Rex Thomas swung around to reassure his ears. The others turned more slowly. Without doubt it was the girl who faced them, but her features were changed — they were cold, hard, merciless.

'Beryl!' Thomas whispered, astounded. 'What on earth are you up to? How did you get here?'

'Not much of a miracle, is it?' she asked tartly. 'You master minds spent *your* time following Mr. Clough.'

'Your car outside — the Clayton car, anyway,' Rex Thomas breathed. 'Of course! But, Beryl — '

'Shut up!' she retorted. 'I'll do the talking here.'

She moved to the door and shut it, stood beside Clough as he too held his revolver steady.

'So the great Dr. Brutus Lloyd walks right into a trap, eh?' Beryl asked cynically.

Lloyd smiled urbanely, tracing designs on the concrete floor with the ferrule of his umbrella.

'This — this is the laboratory I saw!' Thomas exclaimed suddenly, gazing around. 'Sure — there are the chairs with the helmets — six of them! But only five scientists — Beryl, what does this all mean?'

'The sixth chair is reserved for Brutus Lloyd here,' the girl said coldly. 'Probably be a seventh for you, Rex. Even an eighth for Professor Eliman, whom I left until last because he is a dangerous man to handle.'

'You — *You* are the brains behind all this!' Thomas stared in dawning horror.

The girl nodded, her eyes frigid. She gazed at Lloyd suddenly.

'You might as well know how far wrong you went, Dr. Lloyd,' she said briefly. 'I knew my stepfather's formula for synthesis from the moment he invented it. I wanted to get at that valuable material on the moon as much as Clough here did.

My stepfather was too conservative. Clough and I got together and decided on a plan.

'I knew, from what my stepfather had told me at different times, that the pooling of several brains can perform what an individual brain can not. It was necessary to work out the scientific details. Simple enough, with the run of my stepfather's laboratory.

'Brains give forth vibrations that can be detected, picked up, and amplified by mechanical means. You see that electro-magnetic instrument over there? When all the scientists are placed in those chairs and vibratory helmets are put on their shaven heads, electric probes go to the seat of their brains.

'They are powerless to move — the whole nervous system is paralyzed — and their individual will is also blanketed by a negative current. Therefore they give up their every scientific brain vibration, which is electrically amplified and recorded in what might be called the brainpan — that circular copper disk.'

140

'Diabolical!' whispered Thomas. 'I've never heard of anything so fiendish!' Beryl's grin was coldly mocking.

'The copper disk gathers all these vibrations into a composite whole — a vast store of individual knowledge made collective,' the girl went on, obviously revelling in her scientific achievement. 'By wearing a vibratory helmet myself, connected to the brainpan afterward, my brain is able to absorb what has gone into it.

'Hence, an affordable new type of space travel can be devised as a start. Vast gold claims can be registered. Between us, Clough and I intend to start a scientific dynasty of our own.'

'In other words, you murdered all the scientists in order to get their knowledge?' Branson demanded.

'No — they are unhurt, but they cannot return because they will give me away. They can be used later — '

The girl smiled grimly. 'Your brain, Dr. Lloyd, will be worth having.'

The little scientist bowed coolly but still remained silent.

'And yours, Rex,' the girl went on viciously. 'You're a good radio engineer; that's why I got engaged to you. I'm doing nothing wrong — only applying scientific knowledge to the problem of progress. I think my subjects get terrified — but physically they are unhurt. I was somewhat reluctant to use my stepfather too. But then, he is so clever!'

'Where is he now?' Branson snapped. 'You can't get away with this, and you know it!'

'In there,' Beryl said dryly, as there came a desperate hammering on an adjoining door. 'Along with the four supposedly dead scientists and Clough's sculptor friend, Crandal. My dear stepfather worked from the details I supplied him, along with photographs. Nice quiet place here, and some of Clough's men are always on guard.'

'Same men who tried to kill Dr. Lloyd and me tonight, I suppose!' Thomas snapped.

'Exactly.' The girl twirled her revolver menacingly for a moment, then she said briefly,

'As a detective, Dr. Lloyd, you disappoint me! When you telephoned Clough tonight, I had of course phoned him in between and told him what to expect. He answered according to my directions.

'I decided to let you come this far, so that I could use you without having to burden Clough with more kidnapping work, which is difficult and dangerous. In any case, your voice would have given you away. It is hardly like mine!'

'Alas!' Lloyd sighed, shrugging.

'What caused the trouble at my home tonight was the accidental discovery of the body in the laboratory by Parker,' the girl finished. 'To keep up appearances I had to let Parker summon the police.'

'I'll raise hell over that bungling,' Clough growled. 'Leave it to me, Beryl.'

'*Varium et mutabile semper femina* — ever a fickle and changeable thing is woman,' Lloyd commented sadly. 'And to think that *I* of all people should — *do this*!' he finished abruptly; and before anybody present had the least chance to fathom his action, he whirled his umbrella around with tremendous force, spurting a fine choking spray from the umbrella tip.

In an instant Beryl and Clough fired their revolvers helplessly, but the shots went wide. Gasping, choking for air, they dropped to the floor.

'I'm blind!' Beryl screamed, clawing at her face. 'You fiend! You devil!'

Clough was too full of coughing to speak. Inspector Branson hauled him to his feet, clapped the bracelets on his wrists. Without ceremony he did the same to the girl. She stood quivering with fury and fright, drenched in spray, her eyes roving wildly.

'Don't worry, you'll both see all right in an hour,' Lloyd commented briefly. 'Weak solution of an acid I invented myself. Quite a lot in this umbrella shaft — All right, you men, get that door open.'

The connecting door was unbolted immediately, and out of it trooped four haggard, totally bald men. Behind them came weary Dr. Clayton and the small foxy figure of Crandal, the sculptor.

'Brian!' Rex Thomas shouted hoarsely,

clutching the foremost man. 'Brian, it's you!'

Brian Thomas nodded slightly, obviously too exhausted for words.

Clayton stopped in front of Lloyd and said quietly:

'I always suspected — but I never quite *knew*.' He looked at the now passive, haggard girl unhappily. 'It was because of her that I refused to proceed with ideas that might have fostered criminal notions in her brain.'

'You don't have to tell me,' Lloyd murmured. 'I'm only too well aware of it.'

'But you suspected Professor Eliman!' Branson cried. 'You said so!'

Lloyd gave his insolent smile. 'I stand as a supreme brain, Branson — a specialist. I gathered the following points: A — Beryl was not at ease when I purposely mentioned her real last name — Kimberley; B — Professor Eliman, had he been the culprit, would never have lifted scalpels from Dr. Clayton's laboratory, therefore the only other person was Beryl.

'C — Beryl was not even shocked when

I slashed a finger off an apparent corpse of Dr. Clayton, where a normal girl would have gone weak in the knees; D — she had the chance to know everything her stepfather had ever planned or invented; E — she deliberately tried to substantiate my purposely false accusation of Professor Eliman.

'Lastly — F, her mother, Janet Kimberley, went to the State Penitentiary for murder in the first degree. Commuted to life sentence. Sorry, Clayton, but it's true.'

'Yes — it's true,' Clayton muttered.

'It was possible the girl might have carried on the same trend in a more modern way,' Lloyd went on. 'In various ways, besides those I have pointed out, she proved it. I purposely threw her off her guard so that I could see where the victims had gone. So, Branson, don't ever dare to question my genius again!'

Inspector Branson was staring blankly. 'Hell, I don't know where you picked up all that!'

'I gave you a broad hint when I mentioned Beryl's mother. You could have traced her record from police records. I did — spent a whole afternoon doing it, though I'd known the relationship for some time. You, Clayton, married Janet Kimberley when Beryl was three, and thus became her stepfather. To save her daughter, who had taken your name, Janet Kimberley never revealed her own name was Clayton. Right?'

'Right,' Clayton nodded. 'That, I fancy, was the only decent spark Janet ever had.'

There was a brief silence, then Dr. Brutus Lloyd pushed his Derby in place and reset his umbrella.

'Tough luck, Mr. Thomas,' he said, not unkindly. 'But you're young — you'll find another girl.' Then he turned to glare at Inspector Branson.

'Well, what are you waiting for? Let's go! And next time you're in a mess, remember me — *magnum in parvo*, my friend — a great deal in a little space!'

3

THE MESOZOIC MONSTERS

1

Monstrous sightings

'Lloyd! Damned glad you could make it!'

Inspector Branson caught Brutus Lloyd by the arm as he stepped from the 3:10 and led him into the waiting room. The little scientific detective took off his Derby and held it to the fire.

'Either give a good reason for this rush-trip or write yourself off the New York police force,' he growled in his bass voice. 'Just what in hell did you mean over the phone by — *monsters?*'

'What I said! Monsters! Prehistoric things ... They belong definitely to science so I sent for you.'

Lloyd's keen little eyes sharpened. 'You don't mean the things mentioned in an obscure corner of this morning's papers? Creatures from the Mesozoic Era?'

'Just that,' Branson acknowledged bluntly. 'The sheriff here is all steamed over the

151

business — right out of his depth. He sent for help from New York. Having nothing particular on hand I came over. Dinosaurs, Lloyd — that's what!'

Lloyd sighed. 'Dammit man, dinosauria died out millions of years ago — and even supposing otherwise they'd sure have more sense than choose a dump like Trenchley to park in! Anyway, let's have it — and be brief!'

'Better come with me in the car,' Branson said, and led the way outside the station. Then as he drove along the wet roadway through the wildest of drizzling, lonely country to the village of Trenchley itself he spat out laconic statements, mainly embellishing the unimaginative newspaper reports.

'Seems a group of villagers, residents, saw two dinosaurs on the outskirts of the village last evening. I've questioned them all, and they all have the same story.'

'*Deceptio visus* — optical illusion,' Lloyd sneered, too wet and uncomfortable to be interested. 'And anyway dinosaurs cover a whole range of animals — but that would be way above your head of course . . . Village gossip, Branson!'

'I don't think it is!' the Inspector insisted. 'They're sensible people, all of 'em. A young electrical engineer and his wife; a travelling salesman; a clergyman; one or two members of the local church, and — yes, another guy. A spiritualist.'

'Huh?' Lloyd looked up sharply.

'A Dr. Phalnack — plays around with tambourines in the dark and puts the jitters in village folk o' nights. You know the type. Odd-looking chap. He has an Indian servant I didn't like the looks of. Sort of dark, anarchistic guy with a towel round his head.'

'Hmm.' Lloyd fingered the J-shaped forelock poking under his uptilted Derby. Then he sneered, 'I presume you looked for clues?'

'Sure — and I found 'em. Dinosaur's footmarks.'

Lloyd rubbed his tiny hands together. 'That's better! This begins to smell more like my meat.'

Branson looked gratified; then he glanced ahead. 'We're coming into the village now. I asked the folks — the principal ones anyway — to gather in the village hall to meet you. They ought to be there by now.'

He swung the car off the main road into a gravel way, pulled up before a beetle-like tin-roofed shed. In a moment he and Lloyd were inside the place. Walking in slowly behind the burly Inspector the diminutive investigator glanced over, and appraised, the assembly.

There was a young man with an eager, intelligent face and a dark starry-eyed girl by his side. There was the vicar, calm and pale-faced; the waiting Sheriff, chewing thoughtfully; then a smallish man with immensely thick-lensed glasses, cape, and broad brimmed soft hat. Beside him, arms folded, was a Pathan, smouldering-eyed, high-jowelled, turban wound flawlessly round his head. He was short, too — but lithe and muscular as a steel spring.

Branson rattled off the introductions, and the first one to come forward was the man with glasses and broad-brimmed hat.

'I'm so glad to know you, Dr. Lloyd!'

154

His voice was soft, persuasive; and his handgrip crushing. 'I've heard of you, of course.'

'That's understandable!' Lloyd regarded him under insolently lowered eyelids. 'Am I not the master of scientific mystery?'

'Quite — quite! I am Dr. Phalnack, a spiritualistic medium. Oh, this is my servant and confidant, Ranji . . . '

The Indian gave a slight inclination of his head, but his eyes still glowered dangerously. Lloyd peered at him archly from under his upthrust hat brim; then he turned aside sharply as the young man and woman came forward. He was lanky, loose-jointed of movement.

'I'm Ted Hutton,' he volunteered. 'This is my wife Janice.'

'Uh-huh,' Lloyd acknowledged impatiently. 'But suppose we get down to matters? This talk of monsters — '

'It ain't just talk,' Sheriff Ingle snorted. 'I saw the danged things meself . . . We all did. And plenty more besides.'

'True,' agreed the vicar mildly. 'I was calling on Mrs. Westbury concerning the needy children's charity when I saw two huge monsters against the sunset, just outside the village. They seemed to be coming towards me. I — ahem! — moved precipitately into Mrs. Westbury's and sought sanctuary — '

'Then?' Lloyd snapped.

'I — er — Well, I guess they'd gone when I came out some thirty minutes later.'

Ted Hutton put in earnestly, 'I saw them as I was coming back from an electrical survey just out of the village. I'm with the Government, you see — research engineer. And my wife saw the things too, didn't you, sweet?'

'Gigantic!' she declared earnestly. 'Dinosaurs . . .'

The lean-faced man in the dripping mackintosh who called himself Murgatroyd came forward.

'Guess I saw them as I was driving into the village; I'm a salesman, putting up here for a few days.'

Lloyd fondled his forelock and glanced at Dr. Phalnack. 'And you, doctor?'

'Well, I didn't actually see them, I'm afraid — but I certainly knew through my psychic experiments that there was a foreign power close to us — something, if you understand me, otherworldly!'

'We don't!' Branson said, irritated. 'Talk plain English!'

'I was aware of an unwanted dangerous element,' Phalnack elaborated. 'It disturbed my communion with Beyond. The nearest way I can describe the interruption is that it resembled a thin, irritating hum.'

'What the heck!' Branson stared blankly.

'Imitate it,' Lloyd ordered.

Phalnack shrugged and doubled for a wasp. Lloyd eyed him very gravely then glanced at the others. 'Any of you hear that?'

'I was so surprised I don't remember,' said the Sheriff.

'I can't be sure,' Janice Hutton said. 'I had the radio on, you see — at least I was trying to, but something must have been wrong with the battery for there was very bad static — '

'There was a wind so I wouldn't know,' her husband interrupted her shrugging. 'But those monsters existed alright!

Besides, there are the prints!'

'And when were they found?' Lloyd asked.

'Took me to find them,' Branson said with pride. 'I always begin a search at the beginning — '

'Wise of you,' Lloyd grunted. Then, 'Let's go take a look at 'em before it gets dark. All of you,' he added. 'I might want to ask some questions.'

Branson led the way out into the main street, marched with determined strides to the soggy fields just beyond the village. Here, except for the village back of it, the landscape was sheer country, broken only by distant outcroppings of a fairly dense wood . . .

'A monster or two might hide in those woods,' Branson pointed out. 'We can look later — What's the matter?'

Lloyd turned sharply. 'Sorry — I was just admiring the village gaslights.'

'Gaslights?' Branson puzzled; then shrugged. 'Here are the prints.'

Lloyd frowned down on a massive four-toed print in the sloppy mud. There was no denying that a monster possessing

158

such a foot must by proportion have measured at least twenty feet high.

'And here — and here,' Branson indicated, moving further on — until altogether they had covered a mile.

'And leading back to the wood!' Dr. Phalnack observed. 'That seems pretty conclusive, doesn't it?'

'*Non sequitur* — it does not follow,' Lloyd replied sourly. 'And I would point out I require no aid in this matter, Dr. Phalnack. I am Lloyd — therefore self-sufficient.'

He stopped and stared at one of the prints carefully, then from it he picked up bits of what seemed to be wood-shredding from the mud. Carefully he put them away in an envelope, then looked around him.

'Is it possible, Dr. Phalnack, that you heard a thin hum at such a distance as this? How far away is your home?'

'Over there.' And Phalnack nodded across the gas-lighted village to a solitary rain-misted residence maybe a mile on the far side of the dwellings.

'Hmm,' Lloyd said, scowling.

'The doctor sahib speaks truth,' Ranji observed gravely. 'It is not well to even question his word — '

'Speak when spoken to!' Lloyd retorted, glaring. 'Do not dare to cross swords with me, or — '

'But honestly, Dr. Lloyd, I'm sure Professor Phalnack is right,' Janice Hutton broke in earnestly. 'He is too — too clever to need to tell falsehoods. His psychic demonstrations — they're amazing!'

'Phony!' Ted Hutton sniffed.

Phalnack's eyes seemed to gleam more brightly for a moment behind the thick lenses, but he said nothing.

'We might follow this trail to the wood anyway and see where it gets us,' Lloyd shrugged. 'Just time before dark.'

They went forward swiftly, found the footmarks ever and again, leading finally into the wet, drizzling wood itself.

'Wait a minute,' Branson said uneasily. 'If we walk right into a pair of sleeping dinosaurs I don't fancy our chances! Better take it easy — '

Lloyd grinned faintly, then looking

160

back at the others, 'We'll split up and search around. See what we can find . . .'
Then as they went in various directions he added to Branson, 'I still don't believe there are any monsters. Something happened to make these folks think so, that's all . . .'

Branson looked his wonder, then turned to prowl along at Lloyd's side. They had hardly moved a dozen yards in the undergrowth before they were arrested by a gasping scream. It was followed by the unmistakable voice of Ted Hutton.

'Help, quick! Somebody — !'
Instantly the various members of the party converged through the bushes upon the spot where Ted Hutton was standing white and shaken, glancing about him. His wife was holding his arm tightly.

'Ted dearest, whatever's the matter?'
'I — I don't know.' He hesitated, looked around. 'There's something awful in this place,' he breathed. 'An evil power — or something!'

'I understood we were searching for dinosaurs,' Lloyd murmured.

'Yeah, sure we were — But there's something else, invisible! I was ahead of Janice when something I couldn't see got hold of me! I felt as though something were trying to drag me down then — then it went away.'

'So,' Phalnack murmured, pondering, 'my own conclusions of an evil presence were not far wrong perhaps.'

'Bunk!' observed Branson with healthy candour; but he went to search just the same. He came back shrugging.

'Anyway, the trail's lost in this undergrowth,' he growled.

'You remark on an evil presence, doctor,' Lloyd said, turning to him thoughtfully. 'Could you, for instance, really detect an evil power if it were present?'

'Certainly — but I'd have to start a séance.'

'Tonight?'

'Why yes, if you wish.'

'Mainly because the monsters, if any, are likely to appear at night, and also because the forces of evil are more pungent at night,' Lloyd embellished.

'We'll get some tea, then come along to your home around seven-thirty. Right?'

'I'll be honoured,' Phalnack said.

'In fact,' Lloyd added, glancing round, 'it might help if we all went . . . '

'I'm more than willing,' Janice Hutton said eagerly. 'I was so glad when the Government moved Ted up here because it meant I could attend Dr. Phalnack's séances. I first heard of him in the papers, you know, and — '

'You can count me out anyway,' Ted growled. 'This holding hands in the dark is a lot of hooey!'

'Ted!' Janice pleaded.

He sighed. 'Oh, all right. I've been before, so I guess it won't hurt to go again — but you'll never convert me. I'll come this time if only to find out what attacked me . . . ' He broke off and regarded his watch. 'Say, I've an electrical job to finish before evening. See you at home, Jan. 'By, folks.'

He went hurrying off and Lloyd looked at the girl curiously.

'An electrical job in a village lighted by gas?' he asked in some surprise.

She smiled. 'That's his way of putting it. The Government sent him here to study the layout for electrical supply to be given to the village. It should have happened years ago, but I guess bureaucracy got in the way.'

'Ah,' Lloyd nodded. 'I get it,'

'I'll come along too,' Murgatroyd said. 'But I must be getting back to my tea — '

'Come along with us,' Lloyd suggested.

'Thanks all the same, but I don't stay in the village. See you all later.'

He, too, went off, and the rest of the party broke up, finally left Lloyd and Branson alone in the gathering dark.

'Queer for a travelling salesman to put up *outside* a village,' Lloyd reflected; then he shrugged. 'Okay, let's get back and dig up some tea . . . '

2

Seance Extraordinary

'You know, I don't get the angle on this,' Branson growled, as they tramped back through the wood. 'How does a séance help find a prehistoric monster or two?'

'That,' Lloyd beamed, 'is what *I* want to find out — '

He broke off, jumped, jerked himself backwards sharply as something whizzed dangerously close to his face. It landed with a thud in a nearby tree.

Astounded, he and Branson stared at it — then the inspector leapt forward and using his handkerchief tugged forth a knife from the bark.

'Looks sort of . . . oriental,' he said, ominously.

Lloyd didn't answer; he raised a hand for silence. There came the momentary cracking of undergrowth away to their left. Instantly Lloyd raced in the direction

165

of the sound, flying like a gnome over bushes, umbrella raised aloft. He left the cumbersome Branson far behind. But fast though he travelled he could not overtake the fleeing attacker.

He stopped at last, breathing hard. He had lost his quarry.

Branson came up, gulping. 'I saw him,' he gasped out. 'Only for a second or two. It was that Indian guy. I saw his turban — Yes, I was right!' he cried, pointing. 'Look there!'

Nearby was the outjutting branch of a tree, perhaps six feet from the ground. Caught against part of its rough bark was a small piece of white fabric.

'And footprints here!' Branson went on eagerly, pointing to the mud. 'The Indian, sure as fate. It's as clear as day, Lloyd! He caught his turban on this branch and a piece ripped off — '

'Um,' Lloyd said, pulling the fabric down and studying it. He reflected, then asked shortly, 'How tall are you Branson?'

'Six foot one. What's that got to do with it?'

'Plenty. You're not touching the branch.

It's a bit higher than you. And that Indian isn't very tall.'

'Irrelevant!' Branson snorted. 'Running makes a man go a lot higher than normal. If I had a turban on and were to run under this tree — What in hell are you grinning at?' he broke off sourly.

'Just picturing you in a turban! *Res est sacra miser*, Branson — a man in distress is a sacred object . . . But skip it for the moment and let me have that knife.'

Branson handed it over, looking disappointed. 'Look, that was a deliberate effort to kill you. We ought to do things to that Ranji guy.'

'At the séance tonight we probably will,' Lloyd answered. 'Right now I want my tea. Come!'

★ ★ ★

In the local apology for an hotel Lloyd spent a lot of time thinking after he had had his tea. Then finally he pulled out the oriental knife and studied it carefully. He nodded at length.

'Excellent fingerprints. Just what I

need. A few more to tally will help . . . '

Reverently he picked up his Derby hat and to Branson's amazement slipped a tight fitting rubber cover round the brim.

'What the heck?' Branson demanded, round his pipe.

'Rubber, coated with a special solution,' Lloyd beamed. 'The merest touch leaves fingerprints and rain cannot eliminate them. You gaze on a supreme scientist, Branson!'

'I've heard that before. If you're so supreme suppose you tell me how far you've gotten up to now? First we look for monsters, then we make an appointment to sit in the dark and hold hands. We're getting just a bit too old for that!'

'The monsters,' Lloyd said, with his most arrogant glare, 'do not exist. Only the feet exist — and they're made of wood!'

'What!'

Lloyd shook the wood shreddings from the footprint out of their envelope.

'Let us consider,' he said slowly. A — a flat board cut out to resemble a monster's foot would leave the right impression. B

— but whoever did it forgot that the mud would cling to the board and drag off bits of the surface. Obviously rough wood was used. C — a monster, or even a human being, when running or moving swiftly, leaves deeper imprint at the toe end than the heel end. Yet those footprints were level both ends! D — a monster of the dinosaur genus would weigh in the neighborhood of twenty tons. Therefore in soggy soil like it is around here a depression of an inch is absurd. It should be around four to six inches! Lastly — a dinosaur belongs to the saurian or alligator class, so why in heck should it want to choose *land*? It was a water beast mainly . . . The whole set-up smells!'

Branson ran his pipe-stem along his jaw. 'Sounds logical . . . But everybody saw the monsters!'

'That,' Lloyd admitted, 'has me stymied at the moment. But a supreme brain is never baulked. I hope to get it clearer after the séance tonight. Phalnack's 'evil presence' angle rather interests me. A curious sort of guy — and it's possible he may be *actually* psychic: we've no proof

169

otherwise. Anyway, he's got to be fitted into the picture — And it's time we were going.'

'And probably get our throats cut,' Branson growled, buttoning up his coat. 'After this afternoon I'm putting nothing past that Ranji anarchist.'

Muffled to the ears they tramped through the gas-lighted village street to the psychic's home, were admitted by Ranji in person. Lloyd handed over his hat with a gloved hand — then just as quickly snatched it back from Ranji's grasp.

'What am I thinking of!' Lloyd gasped. 'That I should part with my Derby! Huh! Must be wool gathering.'

'This way, gentlemen,' the Indian invited, with steely calm — and glided to a curtained lounge. The rest of the party — the vicar, Ted and Janice Hutton, Murgatroyd, and the Sheriff — were already present, seated in a semicircle on hardwood chairs and gazing at the ornate table and falderals of the doctor's seat of operations.

Lloyd nodded to them and sat down

— then Branson eyed him as he snapped off the rubber band from his hat brim and put it carefully away. He had just done it when Dr. Phalnack came in, attired now in a flowing gown with comets and stars embroidered all over it.

His odd eyes peered through the dense spectacle lenses. With his black brimmed hat off he seemed all head — and that as bald as an egg. Ranji took up a position to one side of him, folded his arms and surveyed the assembly dispassionately. The smell of incense began to fill the air.

'Lights,' Phalnack said softly, sitting down — and they went out. Then his face was thrown into relief by a rosy glow from a hidden globe in the table.

'You will hold hands,' he requested, 'so that the chain of mediumship will not be broken. Mr. Hutton, you will take my left hand; you, Murgatroyd, will take my right. That completes the circle. If there are evil presences around us — or indeed anywhere within five miles — they will be detected. Now, hold hands, please!'

The assembly obeyed, Branson clutching Lloyd's tiny palm and Lloyd himself holding onto the vicar. For a long time there was deathly quiet, except for the wind moaning behind the thick black draperies — Then there came a horrible strangulating gasp from where Phalnack sat. It ended in a sobbing, soul-freezing groan.

'What's he doing — throwing a fit?' Branson whispered uneasily.

'Going into a trance!' Janice Hutton hissed. 'Ssssh!'

'*Quantum mutatus ab illo*,' Lloyd murmured. 'How changed from what he was!'

But at last the howling anguish ceased and there came into the room a faint humming sound, so inaudible one felt rather than heard it. Branson felt Lloyd stiffen intently.

'Evil presence — show yourself!' Phalnack droned.

Surprisingly enough, things did show themselves — but not evil presences. There were tamborines and trumpets. They banged and they blew. Then they gave place to other things, moving diaphanous objects that swept with gossamer unreality through the heavy dark. Faces began to leer out of the void — unpleasant, rascally faces —

'No! No! I cannot go on!' Phalnack screamed suddenly. 'Evil power is present! I cannot — '

Lloyd hurtled suddenly to his feet, flung himself at the nearest floating face to seize it. But instead he went flying — and the abrupt return of the lights found him bundled into a corner, rubbing his head where it had hit the wall.

'I apologize, doctor,' he said gravely, getting up. 'I thought those manifestations were phony — But they're not. No solidity to them.'

'I am a true psychic subject,' Phalnack answered calmly. 'It is a pity you should have ever doubted it.'

'You actually mean these things we saw — tamborines, faces, and what-have-you — were not tricks?' Branson demanded.

'They were not solid anyway,' Lloyd said; then he glanced round. 'Hm — so you have electric lights in a gas-supplied village, doctor?'

'My own generators.'

'Ah . . . ' Lloyd pondered a moment, then, 'I think I heard that thin waspish hum you mentioned during the séance.'

Phalnack shook his bald head quickly. 'That was not the evil influence I told you of: it was purely the normal establishment of psychic contact. But there is an evil presence here just the same! It baulked my efforts.'

'It's a pity it broke up the party,' Lloyd sighed, putting on his Derby again. 'Thanks all the same, Phalnack — it was good while it lasted.' He turned to the Sheriff. 'I've a few things to check up but I'll be back tomorrow. 'Night everybody.'

★ ★ ★

Out in the fresh air Branson gave his big form a violent shake.

'Uh! That place gave me the jitters!'

'And yet it was a valuable experience,' Lloyd commented. 'I got what I hoped to get — the first foundations of a solution. That Phalnack is an extremely clever man, Branson!'

'Struck me as an out and out phony!'

'But nobody, unless he were a scientist, could prove him a phony!' Lloyd said modestly. 'Those manifestations of his were not done with the usual occult trickster's gadgets, such as wires and things. No, they were done by the *mind*! I'll prove it later, too. Right now we're getting back home.'

They returned to the village hall and Branson's car, started out into the dark country road citywards. The rain had ceased now and the moon was shining through ragged clouds.

'A bit odd that a spiritualist of Phalnack's accomplishments should be content to do his stuff in so lonely a spot,' Branson reflected. 'You'd think he'd get busy in a city, frisking devotees of the upper classes.'

'Unless this is his initial experiment and he'll move later,' Lloyd replied; then suddenly he shook his head a little and jabbed a finger irritably in his ear.

'Do you hear something?' he demanded finally. 'I thought I'd gotten bells in my ears. Now I'm not sure if — '

'Hey, will you look at that!' Branson

yelled hoarsely, pointing ahead.

Lloyd jerked his head up — and simultaneously swung the steering wheel frantically out of Branson's grasp. He seemed too stunned to act — paralyzed.

For right ahead of them in the dim moonlight was the shape of a monstrous animal. They had time to notice a spined back — then it swung sideways to them as the car went bounding and bumping into a thickly ploughed field. It halted with a jolt.

They scrambled out and raced back to the roadway. But by the time they had reached it the monster had disappeared. There was nothing visible — but there was a faint sound, a dull purring slowly receding into distance.

'Well, *well*?' Branson snapped impatiently, as Lloyd pondered.

'That noise . . . ' he meditated. 'A car's engine — Yes, here are its tracks! Unique sort of tread too — Notice the wet gravel here? Here's our track where we turned off.'

He stooped, pulled a white card from his pocket, and in the light of the moon made a pencil design of the tyre tread.

'So what?' Branson snorted, glancing round the landscape. 'I'm not interested in tyre treads; I want that monster!'

'*Spero meliora* — I hope for better things,' Lloyd sighed. 'The monster doesn't exist, I tell you'. But the tyre tread does! And it is recent — so obviously it was a car following us. Look, *did* you hear a queer sound before the monster turned up?'

'Yeah — sure I did; like a wet finger squeegeeing glass.' Branson had his imaginative moments. 'But the sight of that thing put me right off answering you — '

'Clearly,' Lloyd said, 'the monster was intended to hurl us off the road and involve us in a nasty accident. Thanks to my everlasting coolness in taking the wheel we are still here . . . Hmm, this gets more fascinating as it goes on. And if it was the same monster as seen by the villagers it was a diplodocus. That puts it out of court straight away since the diplodocus is a marsh and water dweller — Come on, back to the car. Sooner we get to my laboratory the better.'

They went back through the field to the car.

Branson said, 'Look, you mean that whoever followed in that car was deliberately trying to bump us off with a phony diplo — doplo — Whatever you called it?'

'Naturally,' Lloyd growled impatiently.

They climbed back into the car, bumped back to the road, and in the glare of the headlamps followed the trail of the unknown car as far as the wet road carried it. Then they lost it on macadam. Lloyd grunted and relapsed into thought. Around midnight they were back in New York.

'What happens now?' Branson asked, as he followed the little scientist through his cozy home to the laboratory.

'Please yourself,' Lloyd shrugged. 'I'll be working for the rest of the night. Maybe you'd better give your brain a rest and come and see me in the morning.'

'Okay!' Branson knew better than take offence, or stay on where he wasn't wanted . . .

3

Monsters Over New York

Branson turned up again at eight the next morning, was admitted to the laboratory to find Lloyd wrapped in his oversize smock and huddled over coffee and toast. A bench was littered with odds and ends, and scientific instruments, testifying to the kind of night he had spent.

'Brain refreshed?' he asked sardonically, glancing up; and added, 'It'll need to be to absorb what I'm going to throw at it.'

'You found something definite then?'

'I am Brutus Lloyd! Have some coffee . . .'

And as Branson helped himself Lloyd went on, 'The hatband fingerprints and those on the oriental knife don't tally. It was not the Indian who threw the knife at me in the wood. Not that that is any surprise to me. Remember the tree branch? The Indian is only shortish — he could not, despite your fanciful ideas of leaping into the air with a turban on, have hit his head on that branch. It was somebody taller, posing as him.'

'Whom?'

'I don't know, you damn fool! Might be anybody we've met — even Phalnack himself, who though short is taller than Ranji. Or, it may be somebody we have not yet encountered. Once I've found who owns the prints on the knife I'll get some place — For the moment we can skip that. What really is of interest is the solution of the monsters.'

'You've got it?' Branson cried eagerly, and was rewarded with a droop of insolent eyelids. Then Lloyd swung off his high stool and crossed to the complicated apparatus he'd assembled on his workbench. Now as Branson looked at it closely he decided it was rather like a camera, only it had dynamos attached to it.

Lloyd switched on the power, turned the instrument so it faced Branson. He looked uneasy for a moment but Lloyd grinned his fears away. A thin irritating hum began to pervade the air almost at once.

'Take a look!' Lloyd ordered suddenly — and instantly Branson dropped his coffee cup with a yell and dragged out his revolver. He backed to the wall hastily, fired desperately — three times at the form of a tiger slinking toward him!

The bullets whanged right through it, however — Then, miraculously, the tiger was an ape; then a rabbit; finally a cat! Lloyd switched off and the manifestations vanished utterly.

'What the sweet, suffering hell . . . ' Branson relaxed and mopped his sweating face; then glared at Lloyd as he gave a slow, impish smile. 'What was it, man? Movie film?'

'No — I hypnotized you! A trifle when a brain like mine is pitted against a withered walnut like yours.'

'Hypnotism?' Branson started. 'Now wait a minute — '

'Joking apart,' Lloyd said grimly, 'this business is the most ingenious scientific trick I've struck! It is perfectly clear now

— ignoring the monsters for the moment — that Dr. Phalnack has utilized the method used by Professor Cortell at the British University of Sound Research. Professor Cortell made a thorough research — mainly for discovering how to make cities quieter — into sound problems. He produced an array of decibels ranging from airplane motors to leaves on a windless day . . .

'But he also went deeply into the higher researches of sound and discovered what he tentatively called the 'ultimate vibration'. He suggested it as a war weapon to the British authorities, but it was turned down or else pigeon-holed. That doesn't matter. But it is clear that Dr. Phalnack has used the system for his own psychic demonstrations. You see, Branson, Professor Cortell stated quite accurately that the highest audible sound to the human ear is twenty-five thousand vibrations a second. Anything outside and above it is in the ultrasonic range — '

'But we heard that hum!' Branson protested, trying to grasp the idea.

'No: we *felt* it! Just as certain aids for

the deaf rely solely on an instrument contacting the maxillary bone. Vibration — *not* sound. Anyway, Professor Cortell's instrument generated a wave of twenty-five and a half thousand vibrations a second, and at that pitch it affects the brain-centres. Even as unheard noises — to us that is — can stampede the different hearing range of a herd of animals or flock of birds, so a wavelength of twenty-five and a half thousand vibrations can upset a human brain completely. There Professor Cortell ended his research — but obviously Dr. Phalnack had other ideas about the matter.'

Lloyd pondered a moment before he went on. Then,

'By means of electrical amplification he is able to direct his thoughts into the minds of those who have been semi-paralyzed by that ultrasonic hum. Thereby, unconscious of the fact that their normal power of perception is haywire, they believe what *he* wills they shall believe. Mass hypnotism, Branson. And I know it is correct. Last night at the séance I had an inkling of the truth by the insistence of everybody on a thin hum accompanying their visions of the monsters. I felt ultrasonics might play a part somewheres.

'When it became evident at Phalnack's and the spectral visions appeared simultaneously I dived for them to see if they were solid. When they were not, I suspected hypnotism on a scientific scale. Getting back here I looked up researches into ultrasonics and found Professor Cortell's theory in the files. I duplicated the method — a simple matter of vibrating flanges with air current between them — and produced the desired pitch. I turned it on you and at the same time thought *hard* of a tiger — and the rest of the animals. As I had hoped, a subsidiary electrical beam directed towards you amplified my thoughts to you. Easy enough, for a brain is only an electrical machine. Thought amplification is done any day at the National Physics Laboratory for that matter . . . But don't mix it with telepathy. That *would* be something! This is only plain, but clever, hypnotism.'

'So that's it!' Branson gulped the rest of his coffee from another cup. 'That phony occultist just makes his audience see things, huh? But why? As I said, what's the use of trying out such ideas on a lot of villagers? And anyway, what's the idea of the prehistoric monsters? You've made it clear that *anything* could be induced — so why monsters? What's the motive?'

'There,' Lloyd sighed, fingering his forelock, 'you've got me! But having found the method I don't doubt we'll find the rest — '

He broke off and picked up the phone as it rang sharply. He listened, then tossed it to Branson.

'What!' Branson yelped, after he'd listened for a moment or two; then with a startled, 'Okay, I'll be right over!' he flung the instrument down and turned a dazed face.

'Pterodactyls — over New York!' he gulped. 'Over *my* precinct!'

Lloyd stared blankly for an instant, genuinely astounded for once in his life. Then his little chin set firmly. He wheeled round and tore off his smock, bundled into his coat.

'Come on — let's go!' he shouted to the half stunned Inspector; and with that he recovered and raced after Lloyd's hurrying form. Outside they each went to their own cars. Then with siren blaring noisily Branson led the way through the city streets into the precinct where he held sway — but on the outermost edges of it he began to slow down as he became aware again of that hum that was felt rather than heard.

Lloyd's roadster drew alongside. Both he and Branson looked about them. People on the sidewalk were staring up into the morning sky, astounded — some of them frightened. Certainly there was a flock of birds circling up there — monstrous bat-like objects flying in and out of the lofty buildings.

'Same stunt — more power,' Lloyd summed up tensely. 'That hum has got us, man. Force yourself against it — '

'But how? Unless I stop my ears — '

'No dam' good! It's inaudible sound. That's what is so smart about it. Got the people too from the look of 'em. Use your will power, man — what there is of it!'

'Yeah — I get it!' But Branson had an obvious struggle with himself to drive onwards. So for that matter had Lloyd himself though he'd never have admitted it.

Somehow they managed to keep going and by the time they'd gained the precinct headquarters the flying monsters had gone from the sky. People were moving again, talking excitedly to one another.

Confused, bewildered, Branson floundered after Lloyd into the private office.

'Get busy,' Lloyd ordered curtly. 'Have all traffic from this section of the city barred on its way out of the city There's a chance the culprit we want will try and get out of New York — and we're going to stop him! Go on.'

'But what's the use of — ?'

'Get on that phone!' Lloyd yelled, slamming his umbrella on the desk emphatically. 'Time's precious, you dope!'

Branson obeyed; then looked at Lloyd in puzzlement. His little face was puckered.

'We can consider the facts,' he mused, pushing up his Derby. 'A — whoever's back of this knows you are on the job and knows your precinct, therefore the act was staged in your area. Maybe as an effort to convince you that the monsters are real by providing so many other witnesses of them. B — our unknown friend used pterodactyls no doubt so they'd be up in the air and beyond examination; and also to avoid having to leave traces for later study — as in the case of the wood-made footprints. C — a vast increase in the power of the mass-hypnotism is evidenced, for to get so many people under the influence for even a short time points to plenty of juice. And D — that car which followed us last night was obviously heading this way.'

'Then,' Branson said, 'he must have come here for other reasons than to upset me. He no doubt figured he'd disposed of both of us!'

'Unless he came here to be certain of his work . . . '

Lloyd began to pace up and down, clutching his forelock savagely. 'Dammit, there must be a motive behind this monster business, but I can't figure what it is! *At spes non fracta* — but hope is not yet crushed! Right now our job is to find a car with the particular tyre tread of last night. Let's be off.'

They hurried outside, Branson to his squad car and Lloyd to his roadster. In three minutes they were threading their way through the busy city traffic, Branson clearing a track with the siren. Presently speed cops moved up in front and assisted him.

Lloyd, a little way behind, sat thinking as he drove swiftly along — thinking so much he had to put the brakes on suddenly several times. Then he looked ahead of him uneasily as the road seemed to shift horribly before his vision. At the same moment an uneasy tickling sensation burned his throat. Blurred of eye, dazed, he could scarcely see where he was going.

He glanced down, alarmed now at the vision of curling vapour coming up through the car floorboards, enveloping him. He gave a strangled cry, fell back helplessly in his seat. Uncontrolled, his car slewed round in a wild half circle, slammed into a taxi, then rebounded and drove its gleaming radiator into a lamp standard . . .

Lloyd returned to consciousness to find his shirt open and collar loosened while brandy was still searing his throat. He opened his eyes to a doctor's surgery, then beheld the doctor himself and a burly police officer.

'What the — ?' He sat up with a jerk, winced at unexpected bruises. 'What the devil happened?' he demanded aggressively.

The officer answered, 'Guess somebody made an attempt on your life, Dr. Lloyd. You were lucky to get away with it! Some wise guy had fixed a small gas bomb under your brake pedal. When you put the brake on the bomb was crushed and the fumes escaped. The rush of wind stopped them doing serious injury to you, though — '

'And my car?' Lloyd got groggily to his feet, fumbled with the collar the doctor handed him.

'Smashed badly. It's in the Excel Garage — '

'*Hic labor, hoc opus est,*' Lloyd growled in fury, scrambling back into his big overcoat and clutching at his Derby.

'This is the labour, this is the toil! Where's Branson, anyway? How long have I been unconscious?'

'About an hour, sir. Inspector Branson is back at his headquarters if you — '

'Quick — drive me to him. It's urgent! Oh — and thanks, doctor. Send the bill in — Brutus Lloyd. All know me.'

He whisked outside with the officer to the waiting car and inside a few minutes was back in Branson's precinct headquarters. The Inspector looked relieved when he saw him.

'Lloyd! Thank goodness you're okay. I was afraid — '

'Be damned to that! What are you doing here? I thought I told you to stop all traffic!'

'Sure — but that was over an hour ago. I couldn't hold things up indefinitely until you recovered so I — '

Lloyd slammed his gamp down savagely on the desk. 'Did you find what we were looking for? That tyre tread?'

'Well, searching the tyres of some hundreds of cars isn't easy.' Branson scratched his bullet head. 'But I found one that might have been it: you had the pattern card so I couldn't be sure. It was a grey truck, streamlined. Nothing we could pin on the driver, though. Clean licence and so on — But I took a print of his tyres for confirmation.'

'Hm! What did he look like?'

'Middle aged apparently, mustached, cap, scarf — '

'And what happened to the truck?'

'We let it go with the rest of the traffic — but I had tabs kept on it. It was followed but did nothing suspicious. Went round some of the streets then retraced into New York and stopped finally outside the *Evening Clarion* offices.'

'Then?' Lloyd insisted.

'What is this?' Branson asked irritably. 'We couldn't keep on tagging it when it was harmlessly occupied. We let it go — But I took the licence number.'

Branson stopped at Lloyd's cold glare, then tossed down the tyre tread impression card on the desk, together with the license number. Lloyd compared the former with his own card, took off his hat, then tore savagely at his J-forelock.

'And you let the car go!' he groaned. '*Hiatus valde defiendus!* A deficiency greatly to be deplored! Fool! Imbecile! It's the very truck we want! Don't you understand, man? He must have had portable ultrasonic equipment in that truck and produced those pterodactyls — and the monster we saw on the country road last night — by that method!'

'But the driver was a stranger!' Branson shouted hotly.

'Naturally,' Lloyd sneered. 'The guy we want was probably *inside* that truck — but that wouldn't occur to your clogged brain.'

Branson looked uncomfortable. Lloyd drummed his fingers on the desk irritably for a time.

'The motive?' he reiterated. 'Just what can be the sense of throwing a fright into people this way? It doesn't even — Did you say the *Evening Clarion*?' he broke off sharply. 'Which department?'

'Classified advertisements.'

'Hmm . . . ' Lloyd cooled off a little. 'Maybe we'll find something when the

193

paper comes out. In the meantime we have work to do. I have got to find the tallying fingerprints to those on the oriental knife; and since it was not the Indian we've to check on Phalnack himself. Guess we'll grab some lunch, then motor over to Trenchley and wait for nightfall. Soon be dark this time of year.'

4

Trail's End

Lloyd was right. The short autumnal day had closed into frosty night when they parked the squad car outside the village near Phalnack's isolated home. Silently they moved toward it in the gloom.

'I suppose you know you're figuring on burglary — anyway house-breaking?' Branson asked grimly. 'Can't investigate without a warrant.'

'But I can,' Lloyd retorted. 'And I'm going to! None can baulk the will of Brutus Lloyd. You can arrest me afterwards for trespass if you like. Here we go . . . '

They had come to the rear of the sombre residence. With his penknife he opened a window and they slid silently into a gloomy, deserted library. The whole place was deathly quiet, apparently deserted.

They made their way out to the hall, then knowing the set-up from the previous night's visit headed towards the room where the séance had been held. Lloyd moved slowly across to the table from where the demonstration had been controlled by Phalnack. He pulled out a torch, dimmed the light with his fingers, and gave a low chuckle.

'Here we are, Branson! A small ultrasonic instrument. What a brain I've got! Amazing isn't it?'

'Incredible,' Branson agreed, sourly.

Lloyd pulled some powder from his pocket and sprinkled it on the smooth arms of the chair. Instantly fingerprints came into view —

Then something else happened. A silk-clad arm came out of the shadows and closed under Lloyd's chin and round his neck. He gave a yelp and struggled violently, but the arm increased with steely tension, forcing him backwards — So he relaxed abruptly, then jerked forward, flinging up his hand. With a violent ju-jitsu movement he dislodged the hold and lashed out with his tiny fist. It made little effect —

But Branson was on the job now, lunging out with ham-like paws. Gasps and grunts came from the gloom, then as a knife flashed wickedly Branson yanked out his revolver.

'Drop it!' he barked. 'Drop it, or I'll let you have it!'

The knife fell to the carpet. Panting Latin curses Lloyd stumbled to the wall and found the light switch. The glare revealed the sullen face of Ranji, his dark eyes flashing.

'I guessed as much,' Branson growled. 'What the hell did you think you were doing?'

'You have no right here!' the Indian shouted passionately. 'They who seek to kill my honourable master must die! You have tried for too long to discredit him! He is a master-medium, en rapport with the unknown — '

'Yeah?' Branson eyed him suspiciously; then he looked up quickly as Dr. Phalnack himself came in, dressed in a lounge suit over which was a silk dressing gown. The napkin in his hand suggested he'd come from the dining room. He stared round him amazedly.

'Why, gentlemen, what is the meaning of this?'

Branson tried to think of a good lawful reason, but there was none. Lloyd simply went on comparing the chair fingerprints with those on the oriental knife he brought from his pocket. At last he straightened up and handed it over.

'This yours, doctor?' he asked quietly.

'Why — yes!' He took it, clearly surprised. 'I lost it some time ago from this very room; from this table in fact. Where in the world did you discover it?'

'You should ask!' Branson said bitterly. 'Somebody tried to kill Lloyd with it yesterday evening — '

'Silence!' Lloyd commanded; then he went on, 'You'll have to forgive this impromptu entry into your home, doctor. Or if you prefer you can have me arrested. Branson here represents the law — I think. You see, I'd something to verify. These fingerprints on the chair are yours of course?'

'Certainly. Nobody else ever uses that chair.'

'Uh-huh.' Lloyd looked at the Indian, and the look was returned with slumberous, vengeful eyes.

'I'm sure there is some mistake here,' Phalnack said. 'Ranji naturally is concerned for my safety but he wouldn't try to kill you!'

'You are wrong!' Ranji said hotly. 'These accursed fools are trying to discredit you, doctor! I tried only this morning to be rid of this bumptious little Dr. Lloyd. I saw his car in town outside police headquarters when I went into the city to make your purchases, doctor. It saved me going to his home to settle accounts with him. I hoped I'd kill him — '

'With a gas bomb?' Lloyd asked sharply.

'Why not? I was going to throw it into your home; instead I found a better way. But you still live.'

'Shall I make out a warrant for — '

Branson stopped as Lloyd raised his hand. 'No. Maybe Ranji was under the impression I was out to do Dr. Phalnack here an injury; his fanatical loyalty is rather touching — and illuminating in other ways.'

'I never realized — ' Phalnack started to say; but Lloyd cut him short with a question.

'Naturally you have heard of Dr. Cortell's interesting experiments in ultrasonics?'

'So you have tumbled to my psychic demonstrations?' Phalnack gave a slow, uneasy smile. 'Yes I've heard of him — and elaborated his ideas. I rather feared a scientist like you would grasp the idea. But I am psychic too — to a degree.'

Lloyd expanded at the flattery. 'Tell me, why do you practice your — er — phony art in a lonely spot like this? Why not a city?'

'Later perhaps. To begin with I prefer to test the stunt on unsophisticated people. Ranji, of course, provides 'noises off'.'

Lloyd shrugged. 'Well, what you choose to do with phony spiritualism is no direct concern of mine: the law will handle that. I'm looking for monsters — and I've got all I need here. If you think of pressing the trespass charge remember what this Indian of yours did to me. I'll lodge counter-charges. Good night!'

But in the dark roadway again heading to their car Branson gave a grunt of impatience. 'You crazy, Lloyd? If that Indian tried to have you gassed he sure threw that knife also!'

'Humph!' was Lloyd's illuminating answer.

'Anyway,' Branson said aggrievedly, 'Phalnack must be crazy to admit his ultrasonics that easily.'

'Either that or else he believes like many criminals that the best defence is admission of apparent guilt. As to the knife, it is his and he admits it. But the fingerprints were not his on the knife; nor were they Ranji's.'

'Gloves!' Branson grunted.

'But the fingerprints belong to somebody, you dope . . . ' Then Lloyd relapsed into silence, thinking, clambered back into the car at Branson's side. He turned the car round.

'Where to?'

'Home. I want an *Evening Clarion*.'

Once back in New York Lloyd got the first copy he came across and hurried with it into headquarters beside Branson. Together they went through the classified advertisements carefully, page after page of them. An hour passed; an hour and a half — Then Lloyd gave a yelp.

'*Flammo fumo est proxima!* Where there's smoke there's fire! A possible motive at last, Branson! Listen to this — 'Monsters! Why not insure yourself against possible attack? Small premiums. Absolute cover guaranteed. Write Box 42/2'.'

Branson scowled. 'But what the heck? Who'd want to insure themselves against monsters on the strength of that stunt this morning?'

'Probably dozens of people! Think of the weird things that *are* insured! It's possible after this morning that hundreds of New Yorkers — more nervous ones anyway — may answer this ad., and be willing to pay for supposed safety. That's human nature — and damned clever psychology on the advertiser's part. Later it could build up into quite a racket, especially if monsters — or other terrifying things — reappear! Money for ultrasonics!'

'Lord!' Branson gasped. 'You mean somebody — probably Phalnack — is having the face to create monsters just so he can insure against them? Make money out of premiums, knowing he will never have to pay out anyway?'

'Exactly — a streamlined version of an old insurance racket. Supply a demand: then make the supply. This is where we go to town. Ah, masterful mind that I have! *Ecce homo*, Branson — behold the man! But come — to the *Evening Clarion* offices.'

They were soon there and Branson's official capacity opened Sesame to many things. In a few minutes they had the address of the advertiser — a remote spot in the country, but significantly it wasn't very far outside Trenchley.

'Whoever is the advertiser is our man,' Lloyd said exultantly, as they came out on the sidewalk again.

'Phalnack for sure,' Branson growled. 'This spot is only about a mile from his place. Let's see — Hawthorn Filling Station, Trenchley Main Road. Damned funny spot to have an insurance office!'

'Not if it's worked on the mail order system. Nobody will question the address much as long as they get insurance. An insurance actuary doesn't always have a high class office.'

Branson nodded thoughtfully, then got into the car. For the second time that evening they headed out of New York — and the place they sought demanded a good deal of wandering, of searching by headlamps; then at last they located it. It was a rather decrepit filling station well off the main highway in Trenchley and apparently deserted. Certainly no lights were on. How anybody could hope to keep the business flourishing in such a dead-alive hole was problematical.

'Stop here,' Lloyd ordered finally; and with all the car lights switched off they halted a hundred yards from the garage. Then together they moved towards it. From one window they caught a glimpse of light through an imperfectly drawn shade.

'Here we go!' Lloyd murmured, and suddenly raising his bass voice he bawled, 'Hey there, any gas? Give us some service!'

Instead of a response there were the sounds of shuffling from inside the building and the light snapped out.

'Go for 'em!' Lloyd snapped; and brought his umbrella down on the window with shattering force. Branson was just as quick, thrusting his revolver and torch through the smashed pane, tearing the shade down the centre.

'Hold it!' he ordered, as two figures twirled in the torch beam; then as they slowly raised their hands he began to clamber through —

But the shade got in his way and finally fell on top of him. The two still unidentified men took instant advantage, dodged into the dark, and were gone. Cursing furiously Branson stumbled into the little badly furnished office with Lloyd behind him. They had hardly got themselves disentangled before the sound of a car's engine starting up assailed them.

'They're getting away!' Branson yelled. 'Come on — after 'em — '

Lloyd swung round and bumped into the table. He stopped, seized Branson's torch.

'The evidence!' he exclaimed, and indicated a portable ultrasonic equipment on the table, not unlike the one he had himself devised. 'Probably a small scale model of the one they've got in that truck of theirs . . . Okay, let's go. We've got Exhibit A anyway.'

He whisked it up and they pelted outside to their own car. Lloyd sat with the portable instrument on his knees as the car whisked out of the dark down the solitary road. For safety's sake the fleeing truck had to use its headlights, identifying itself instantly. Branson jammed down the accelerator and tore out onto the main road like a rocket, continued on whistling tires through the dark. His headlights began to show the truck up. It was dove-grey all right, streamlined —

'That's it!' Branson snapped. 'Same licence number!'

Then things began to happen. The road

in front of them started to blur, seemed to shift in two directions. There were two grey trucks now and four sets of headlights! A thin hum was in the air — Branson shook his head confusedly, pinched his eyes momentarily.

'They're using that ultrasonic stuff to ditch us,' Lloyd said quickly. 'But maybe we've a trick left ourselves — !' He began fumbling with the apparatus on his knees, found a power lead and clamped it into the socket usually used for the car radio. Power of sorts surged into the instrument for it glowed. Scowling at it, directing the lens ahead, Lloyd concentrated.

In a moment or two he got results — surprising ones, for the truck went careening off the main road into a field, bounced, turned right over and finished on its side. Instantly they hopped from their own car and chased after it.

'What did you do?' Branson panted, as they ran.

'Same as he did to us! Concentrated on two roads. They didn't know I had apparatus to do the trick and took it as the real thing!'

They'd arrived at the truck now. A figure was crawling from the driving seat; yet another was making frantic efforts to get out of the back doors. Branson went to the front; Lloyd to the back. He paused as he was about to grasp the metal handle on the door and instead yanked a card and powder from his pocket. He gave a grim smile at what he found, then pulled the door open.

It was Ted Hutton who came staggering out, disheveled, a bruise on his head where he'd struck the instruments in the truck.

'Say!' Branson exclaimed, appearing with the other man, 'this guy is Murgatroyd, the travelling salesman. He was disguised with a phony mustache and cap pulled down — Hutton!' he exclaimed, staring at him.

'Hutton,' Lloyd acknowledged grimly. 'And the fingerprints tally with those on the knife. Okay, Branson — the bracelets.'

★ ★ ★

'To sum up,' Lloyd said, towards midnight when he and Branson were at precinct headquarters after taking Hutton's full confession of an effort to launch a super-insurance racket; 'A — I suspected Hutton when I suspected ultrasonics, because being an electrician he would probably know about them. B — his story of being present in the village for Government reasons — in a village with only gaslight — sounded phony. C — he cut his wife short when she said she had bad static on her radio on the night of the monsters. But I was quick enough to see static was impossible in a village devoid of electricity; therefore, the monsters were probably electrical in basic origin. D — his wife made a remark that she'd heard of Phalnack in a newspaper. Hutton knew that too; and as he has since confessed, moved in to Trenchley because he had heard Phalnack was an expert in ultrasonics. He figured, knowing his wife's weakness for spiritualism, that he might get ideas from Phalnack. Which he did . . .

'Then,' Lloyd proceeded; 'we come to Point E. Hutton decided on 'monsters' because their unusual and terrifying nature would be best calculated to scare people into insurance. F — his colleague owned the truck in which he put the equipment; and I suspected Murgatroyd because he lived outside the village. G — Hutton did his best to blacken Phalnack as much as possible, hence his early theft of the oriental knife owned by Phalnack — but in his urgency to throw it he did nothing to save *his* fingerprints getting onto the hilt as well as Phalnack's numerous ones from normal handling of the knife. Phalnack's were blurred and numerous: Hutton's new and distinct. Obviously he'd had plenty of chances to steal that knife at earlier séances. H — the appearance of the monsters in the village was, as Hutton has admitted, his first test. To his consternation it brought me on the job, and he tried to get rid of me by various clumsy expedients. He resorted to the knife, the turban disguise, a make-believe evil spirit in the wood and running us off the road. Accidentally, his 'turban' caught the tree.'

Lloyd sighed, gave a shrug. 'Altogether Branson, an ambitious young scientific adventurer who took the wrong turning

. . . A last word: Phalnack probably is somewhat psychic, even as he said. The evil presence at the séance was doubtless Hutton . . .'

'By and large,' Branson commented, 'we cleaned everything up in fine style.'

Lloyd's eyelids drooped. '*Veni, vidi, vici*,' he growled. 'I came I saw, I conquered. Now get the hell out of here and let me get on with my diatomic culture research!'

THE END

MIRACLE MAN
THE MULTI-MAN
THE RED INSECTS
THE GOLD OF AKADA
RETURN TO AKADA
GLIMPSE
ENDLESS DAY
THE G–BOMB
A THING OF THE PAST
THE BLACK TERROR
THE SILENT WORLD
DEATH ASKS THE QUESTION

We do hope that you have enjoyed reading this large print book.

Did you know that all of our titles are available for purchase?

We publish a wide range of high quality large print books including:
Romances, Mysteries, Classics
General Fiction
Non Fiction and Westerns

Special interest titles available in large print are:
The Little Oxford Dictionary
Music Book, Song Book
Hymn Book, Service Book

Also available from us courtesy of Oxford University Press:
Young Readers' Dictionary
(large print edition)
Young Readers' Thesaurus
(large print edition)

For further information or a free brochure, please contact us at:
Ulverscroft Large Print Books Ltd.,
The Green, Bradgate Road, Anstey,
Leicester, LE7 7FU, England.
Tel: (00 44) **0116 236 4325**
Fax: (00 44) **0116 234 0205**

Other titles in the
Linford Mystery Library:

S.T.A.R. FLIGHT

E. C. Tubb

The Kaltich invaders are cruelly prolonging their Earthmen serfs' lives and denying them the secret of instantaneous space travel, so desperately needed by a barbaric, overpopulated Earth. While the Kaltichs strip Earth of its riches, the Secret Terran Armed Resistance movement, STAR, opposes them — but it's only their agent, Martin Preston, who can possibly steal the aliens' secrets. If he fails, billions of people will starve — with no place to go to except to their graves.

THE SILENT WORLD

John Russell Fearn

Around the world there was total silence from Pole to Pole. Seas crashed noiselessly on rocky shores, hurricanes shrieked mutely across the China Sea. People shouted and were not heard; alarms and bells rang and yet were mute. The dead wall of silence was everywhere — the most strident sound was unable to break through it. Scientists were unprepared for The Silence. There was something amiss with the laws which governed sound — but that was only the beginning . . .

DOUBLE ILLUSION

Philip E. High

Earth — four hundred years from now — a rotten society in which mankind is doomed to die out — and one seemingly average man with incredible I.Q. potential . . . An ultra-intelligent computer is built and used to govern humanity — and all corruption in the world is eradicated. Mother Machine decides what's best for her human children — and it is done. But the all-powerful computer is turning mankind into zombies. The world's only hope lies in one outlawed, not-so-average man . . .